WISH YOU WERE HERE?

Cara was hoping to spend Christmas in England with her boyfriend, but her mother sweeps her off to a holiday home in Spain. However, they are forced to stay in a hotel, wondering if they can afford the bill. There, she becomes attracted to Nick, despite his being ten years her junior. But, unexpectedly, her boyfriend, Geoff, and Nick's girlfriend, Lily, appear at the hotel. Then both Nick's and Cara's fathers add to the complicated network of relationships . . .

SHEILA HOLROYD

WISH YOU WERE HERE?

Complete and Unabridged

LINFORD
Leicester

First published in Great Britain in 2010

First Linford Edition
published 2012

British Library CIP Data

Holroyd, Sheila.
    Wish you were here?. - -
    (Linford romance library)
    1. Love stories.
    2. Large type books.
    I. Title II. Series
    823.9′2–dc23

    ISBN 978–1–4448–1036–3

Published by
F. A. Thorpe (Publishing)
Anstey, Leicestershire

Set by Words & Graphics Ltd.
Anstey, Leicestershire
Printed and bound in Great Britain by
T. J. International Ltd., Padstow, Cornwall

This book is printed on acid-free paper

1

Cara tried to close the skimpy curtains, but they wouldn't quite meet in the middle. She stood for a moment gazing out at the dismal scene. This was Spain, the Costa del Sol, but so far she had seen very little sun. The rain which had been falling all day was still pouring down upon the closely-packed rows of little houses, and the December dusk was making it look still more depressing.

'What are we having for supper?' her mother asked hopefully.

'Well, we still have some salad left.'

'We had that for lunch.'

'There is frozen pizza, or we could have a cheese omelette.'

It was no surprise to Cara when Mrs Dale shook her head.

'They don't sound very exciting. I know! Why don't we pop across to the hotel and have dinner there?'

'Mother, that will be the third night in a row that we have been there.'

'But the food is good, and some new guests were due to arrive today. It's always interesting to meet new people, and we won't have to wash up.'

Cara gritted her teeth. Her mother hated housework and cooking, but loved making new friends, while she preferred a quieter life and could never remember names! Still, she was tired of being cooped up in the small holiday house with nothing to do but gaze out at the miserable weather.

'They may not have room for us. It's only a week to Christmas and the hotel is getting full,' she warned her mother.

Mrs Dale giggled.

'Manuel will always find a table for me.'

'Only because you flirt with him so disgracefully!'

Her mother pretended to take offence.

'I'm just being friendly. Is it my fault that he finds me attractive?'

Most men found Mrs Dale attractive. She was well into her fifties, but her youthful face was unlined under her shining blonde hair, and her large blue eyes were always smiling. She dressed to suit her petite figure and her make-up was unobtrusive but immaculate.

Cara was thirty-five, and knew her own dark hair and eyes were considered attractive by many men. Four inches taller than her mother, sometimes she felt large and clumsy next to her glamorous parent. She wasn't so dedicated to fashion, and quite often did not bother with make-up unless she had to go out, something which her mother deplored.

'Appearance matters,' she would say. 'You are what people see.'

Now Mrs Dale was in her bedroom, rummaging through her wardrobe, selecting what to wear to the large hotel on the seafront, five minutes' walk away. Suddenly she gave a small scream.

'Cara! My black velvet is all wet!'

Cara hurried to investigate the

wardrobe. As her fingers encountered damp cloth her heart sank. She checked the top of the wardrobe. It was dripping wet.

'There's a leak, and the rain is getting in. Fortunately, there's another wardrobe in the spare room, so we'll have to move your clothes there.'

She helped her mother transfer armfuls of clothes, her mouth set grimly. After the fourth trip, she started to complain.

'You seem to have brought all your clothes with you, Mother. No wonder we had to pay extra for our luggage!'

Her mother, carrying one skirt on a hangar, shrugged.

'You never know what will be useful on holiday.'

Cara dumped the last garments on the bed.

'First thing tomorrow I am going to call the agent,' she announced. 'His telephone number is in the information pack. He can deal with the leak — as well as the noise in the pipes and the cracked tiles in the kitchen.'

'We don't want to make too much of a fuss. It might be expensive.'

'The information pack said that repairs were covered by the yearly maintenance charge.' Cara shot a suspicious look at her mother. 'I suppose Father has paid it?'

'I'm sure he sorted it all out,' her mother said with dignity. 'Now, let's go and have dinner.'

They put on jackets, covered their heads with scarves, and hurried through the rain to the hotel.

'At least it's warm rain,' her mother pointed out.

'I know. Everyone says it's the hottest — and the wettest — December they've ever known,' Cara said resignedly. 'I think I'd prefer a little more sun, even if I did have to wear a jumper.'

* * *

The hotel's reception area was bustling with people. Cara and her mother hung up their coats in a cloakroom and made their way to the restaurant, where the head waiter was looking decidedly harassed.

'Can you find us a table for two, Manuel?' Mrs Dale placed a hand lightly on his arm and smiled up at him.

He patted her hand, but shook his head regretfully.

'Even for you, Mrs Dale, I think that is impossible tonight.'

Her face fell. She was not accustomed to failure.

Manuel looked at her apologetically.

'The hotel is nearly full. Perhaps I can persuade someone to let you share their table.'

Without waiting for a reply, he vanished among the people milling round the buffet, and reappeared a minute later wearing an anxious smile.

'There is a lady and her son at a table for four. They have said you can sit with them.'

This was not what Mrs Dale wanted.

'If that's the best you can do, we shall have to accept it,' she replied with a sad little smile which conveyed her disappointment.

'It is very kind of them to let us share their table.' Cara spoke crisply. She was beginning to feel hungry.

Manuel led them to a table in a corner of the room. A middle-aged woman greeted them without enthusiasm when Cara and her mother began to express their gratitude.

'The waiter said there was no other room for you, so we agreed to share,' the woman said resignedly. 'Though one doesn't expect to have to do so at a hotel like this.'

Her son, who looked about twenty-five, had stood up when Cara and Mrs Dale appeared, and gave a cheerful smile that compensated for his mother's cool greeting.

'We were glad to be able to help. Please sit down. This is my mother, Mrs Clarke, and I am Nick.'

'I am Mrs Dale — Paula Dale — and

this is my daughter, Cara.'

They sat down, and the slightly awkward silence between them was broken by Nick Clarke.

'Did you arrive today as well?'

'We came here four days ago, but we're not actually staying at the hotel. We have a holiday home nearby, so we've just come for dinner,' Mrs Dale explained. 'Are you here for Christmas?'

His mouth twisted in a wry smile.

'Yes. We came this morning, and I have already lost count of the number of people who've told us that this wet weather is most unusual, and that we are sure to have sun for Christmas!'

There were sympathetic murmurs. Mrs Dale insisted on ordering a bottle of wine for them all in return for sharing the table, and the atmosphere grew more friendly.

'You are lucky to have a house in this area,' Mrs Clarke commented. 'Do you use it much?'

Mrs Dale's fingers were playing with

the gold chain she always wore around her neck. Cara had realised long ago that her mother had this mannerism whenever she was wondering how to adapt the truth to meet a situation's demands.

'My husband only acquired it recently, and this is the first time we have stayed in it. It's very nice — detached, with three bedrooms.'

Cara reflected that, while it might be technically detached, if you stood between two of the houses and stretched out your arms you could touch both of them. The bedrooms were miniscule, and the garden was really a paved area just big enough to park a car.

'Has it got a swimming-pool?' was Mrs Clarke's next question, and she raised her eyebrows when the answer was in the negative.

'You say your husband acquired it. Isn't he here with you?'

Mrs Dale sighed wistfully.

'I'm afraid not. He hopes to join us

for Christmas, but he is very busy.'

'What does he do?'

'He is an entrepreneur.'

That was one way of describing him, Cara thought. Her father was a wheeler-dealer, always looking for the next opportunity to make money, ready with a new scheme when one failed. During her childhood she had had to accept the frequent sudden changes in their circumstances. Sometimes they'd lived in substantial, elegant houses, only to exchange them at short notice for poky flats until Mr Dale struck lucky again.

Cara had been resigned to the fact that she was always changing schools and therefore never seemed to have a chance to form lasting friendships. Accommodation was always rented fully furnished, and Cara had been unable to think of any of their temporary residences as her home. Her mother seemed to enjoy the constant variety, but as soon as she could, Cara had taken charge of her own life. She'd gone to evening classes to compensate for her patchy education, and had worked her way up through a series of jobs. Now thirty-five years old, she held a responsible post in a bank, and recently had achieved a long-held ambition and bought a small terraced house. Furnished with second-hand pieces from auctions and junk shops it may be, but it was hers, her home.

'And your husband?' Mrs Dale was enquiring in turn.

Mrs Clarke's lips tightened.

'He is no longer with us.'

Nick diverted Cara's attention with some comment on the hotel. She laughed at his remark and attracted Mrs Clarke's disapproving gaze.

'Of course it was very good of Nick to come and keep me company,' she said. 'I'm sure he would much rather be with friends of his own age.' She gave Cara a meaningful look.

So I'm being warned off, Cara thought. Does she think I don't know her son is far too young for me?

Her mother, meanwhile, had leaped to her daughter's defence.

'We are in the same situation. Cara has a gorgeous boyfriend, Geoff, back in England, yet here she is with me. I haven't met him yet, but she's told me all about him.'

Cara thought wistfully of how she had planned to spend the first Christmas in her house quietly, hopefully with Geoff for company most of the time.

'I'm sure we can do that, can't we, Cara?'

Cara woke up from her brief reverie about Geoff, to find her mother looking at her expectantly.

'Mrs Clarke has asked us to stay for the evening's entertainment. That's all right with you, isn't it?'

Clearly, once both mothers had tacitly agreed that their offspring were safe from each other, an armistice had been declared.

When they'd all finished their meal, Mrs Clarke and Nick went ahead to reserve a table in the lounge for coffee, while Mrs Dale produced her credit card to pay for their dinner.

'You're going to have an awfully big bill to pay by the end of the month,' Cara observed, but her mother shrugged.

'Don't worry. Your father will deal with it.'

Cara had heard this many times during her life, and certainly, so far, her father had managed to cope one way or another. She just hoped his luck would hold.

That evening in the hotel the only entertainment on offer was a trio who played tunes — not very well — which had been popular ten years earlier.

'They don't make a huge effort on the first night most guests arrive,' Mrs Dale reassured her companions over coffee. 'After all, most people are tired by their journey, and go to bed early.'

Still, it was pleasant to relax to the sound of the music. A few people began to dance and Nick turned to Cara.

'Would you like to dance?'

She smiled.

'It might encourage the musicians.'

They seemed to fit together naturally as they glided slowly round. Nick was nearly six feet tall and moved well.

'Do you always spend Christmas with your mother?' she asked.

He hesitated a moment.

'Not always,' he said, and then seemed to feel this needed more explanation. 'She lost my father earlier this year, so I couldn't leave her on her own. I decided that a hotel abroad should provide sufficient distraction to stop her remembering other Christmases.'

'That was thoughtful of you — especially as it means you won't be able to meet up with friends.'

He grinned.

'I enjoy seeing my friends, but I can stand a fortnight without them. How about you? Are you missing your boyfriend?'

'Sometimes,' was her reply. 'Settling into the house and looking after Mother

14

hasn't given me much time to think of other things.'

This was not quite true. She was, in fact, hoping that Geoff might follow her to Spain, and she'd been looking out for him every day. She had only just begun her Christmas break when her mother had appeared at her house without warning, in a taxi crammed with luggage, and had announced that she and Cara were going to the Costa del Sol for Christmas.

She'd refused to listen to Cara's arguments.

'Your father is busy, and has got to stop in England for a bit. I can't go to Spain by myself — I'd be so lonely in the house, and you know I wouldn't be able to manage on my own. So you have to come with me.'

It was true Mrs Dale was not domesticated, nor was she practical. Reluctantly Cara accepted her fate and started packing. She had telephoned Geoff to break the news.

'If you want to send me a Christmas

card, this is the address,' she'd told him, and after carefully spelling out the address she'd casually mentioned that the house did have three bedrooms. She didn't want to issue a direct invitation, because a refusal would have been awkward for both of them, but she knew he had no other engagements over the holiday.

She hoped he'd take her strong hint and appear in Spain. If he did, if he was actually prepared to spend a family Christmas with her and her parents, it was symbolic. It would mark a big step forward in their relationship.

Her mother had been vague about the reasons for her husband's absence, but then she had never bothered herself about the details of his activities.

'Your father is very busy and has a lot of places to visit,' was all she had been willing to say.

Cara, surprised to find that her father had acquired a house in Spain, since he'd never bought one in England, had pressed for an explanation.

'He didn't actually buy it.' Her mother's blue eyes opened wide. 'The man who used to own it owed your father money and couldn't pay, so instead he gave him the Spanish house.'

Mrs Dale's preparations for the holiday hadn't included buying air tickets, so it was Cara who'd booked their seats on a budget air line. As her mother was vague about when she wanted to return, she'd bought one-way tickets.

Cara had been relieved, when they arrived on the Costa del Sol, to find the house really existed and was quite acceptable. It had been clean and tidy, ready for occupation when they arrived during a rare interval of sunshine, and she'd actually started to look forward to a few days of swimming and walking.

Then the rain had started!

'If you get bored,' Nick said tentatively now, 'we could do something together. Our mothers seem to be getting on well, so they wouldn't need us hanging around all the time.'

Companionship without the expectation of romance would be very acceptable. Nick was a pleasant-looking young man, and the difference in their ages meant there would be no romantic complications.

'What a good idea!' She blushed. 'I didn't mean to sound so eager, but I've already spent four days gazing out at the rain, and it would be nice to have a little variety.'

'Give me your mobile number before you go, and I'll call you.'

'Right. But not tomorrow morning. I've to get the agent to deal with a leak in the roof.'

He laughed.

'That is one benefit of staying in a hotel! Anyway, tomorrow morning we are going to have the usual talk when we're told about the place and urged to sign up for excursions.'

They went back to their seats and found their mothers drinking more coffee and discussing their favourite television programmes. The lounge was beginning to empty, and Cara suggested that, as the rain had stopped briefly, it might be a good time to go home. Mrs Dale agreed, assuring her new friend that she would see her again soon.

'We quite often drop in here for dinner. It saves me cooking,' she said, while Cara tried to remember when her mother had ever done anything more complicated in the kitchen than fry eggs or microwave ready meals!

Nick saw them to the door, and when they reached the gate Cara saw that he was still standing watching them. She waved, and he waved back. She'd enjoyed the evening with him. She liked his thick dark hair and the way his eyes crinkled when he smiled. But, of course, he was just a boy, and could not rival Geoff!

Back at the house, her mother stretched like a cat.

'This evening was fun,' she announced. 'Mrs Clarke is very pleasant, though she doesn't have much to talk about except herself. Her son looks all right — you'll be safe with him.' She yawned. 'We'd better go to bed. There's the agent to deal with in the morning. I know you are very capable, but if he's awkward I'll use my charm on him!'

It had been an unexpectedly pleasant evening, and that night Cara found herself mentally comparing Geoff and Nick. At least, if Geoff didn't appear, she now had Nick to brighten up her holiday — purely platonically, of course.

2

Early the next morning, Cara looked up the number of the agent who looked after the houses and telephoned, hoping that his English would be adequate, as her Spanish was non-existent. To her relief, not only did he answer immediately but his English was excellent. She gave him the address of the house and told him what repairs needed doing. That was a straightforward matter, and he told her the problems would be dealt with quickly. But he did seem mildly puzzled that she was actually in the house.

'I did not expect you there for another few days.'

'Perhaps my mother decided to come earlier than she had planned — I'm not sure.'

'Yes. Perhaps.'

He still sounded doubtful, and asked

for her name. There was a long pause after she'd spelt it out and then he asked her to repeat it. She did so, patiently. There was an even longer pause before he assured her that he'd come to see the state of the house for himself that afternoon.

She put her mobile away slowly, wondering. Perhaps some small detail had been overlooked when ownership of the house had been transferred to her father, or the agent hadn't been told of the change. Well, she would find out what the problem was that afternoon, and deal with it. Meanwhile, she persuaded her mother that they should take the twenty-minute stroll into the nearby town of Nerja and stock up on food.

They wandered round the pleasant little town, peering into shop windows, and then spent a few minutes gazing out to sea while they enjoyed a cup of coffee. Finally they found a super-market and bought what Cara regarded as necessities. The walk back seemed longer as they were both carrying bags of shopping, and it was made worse when it began to rain again. They were both very relieved to reach the house.

Mrs Dale sank gratefully into a chair.

'My feet are killing me! Make a cup of tea, Cara, and can you turn up the heating? It's cold in here.'

But Cara was standing in the middle of the room, wondering where the draughts were coming from. She went into her bedroom and stopped, her eyes widening in horror. A pane of glass had been smashed, and then someone had obviously reached in to open the window, which had been left swinging loose on its hinges. The intruder had clearly climbed in and searched the room, for her clothes and the rest of her possessions were strewn about the floor and bed.

She ran back into the living room and seized her handbag, fumbling for her mobile phone.

'Did you hear me say I wanted tea?' Mrs Dale said impatiently, and then saw her daughter's face. 'What's the matter?'

'A burglar,' Cara replied. 'Now, what's the Spanish emergency number? Oh, I remember!'

She tapped at her phone and was soon connected to someone who, to her relief, spoke English. She explained the situation, ended the call, and went to her mother, who was already checking her own bedroom. There was less disorder than in Cara's.

'It looks as if whoever it was started in my room, came in here but then heard us coming back and left by the window.' She shuddered. 'They may have still been in the house when we were opening the door! Anyway, the police will soon be here.'

Two uniformed men in fact arrived fifteen minutes later, at the same time as a small, bald man with spectacles who introduced himself as Señor Gomez, the agent. The police were polite and efficient, but clearly thought they could do little except provide documentary evidence for the insurance company. The would-be thief had left no traces, and the Dales were informed with a shrug that there was little likelihood that he would have been stupid enough to leave fingerprints.

The houses around them were empty at this time of the year, so there were no possible eye-witnesses. Fortunately a quick check showed that nothing had been taken except Cara's DVD-player and a few English pounds which she had left in her bedside drawer. Finally, the police took their leave, polite to the end.

The agent stayed. Cara looked at him, puzzled, and then nodded as she remembered her earlier telephone conversation.

'If you come with me, I can show you exactly which repairs need doing.'

He followed her, making notes. But then, instead of leaving or informing them the work would be carried out, he stood in the middle of the floor and announced that there were some matters he needed to discuss with Cara and her mother.

With a sense of foreboding Cara fetched her mother, who was tidying up the bedrooms.

'I was surprised to receive your call,' Señor Gomez said in his careful English. 'I understood that the house would be empty for the next few days, and that then a family named Wilson, who had rented it for two weeks over Christmas, would arrive. Your name is Dale, not Wilson.'

'Rented it?' exclaimed Mrs Dale. 'The house is ours. It belongs to my husband, and he's certainly not rented it to anyone else!'

Señor Gomez pushed his spectacles up his nose, but said nothing.

'Obviously there has been some misunderstanding,' Cara told him. 'The Wilsons must be renting another house.'

He shook his head.

'May I ask if you have any proof of ownership?'

'Indeed I have,' Mrs Dale said triumphantly. 'My husband gave me the letter from a Mr Heywood, the man who owned the house before him.' She went into her bedroom and came back waving an envelope. 'Here it is! Mr Heywood promised to send the official documents to his solicitor.'

Señor Gomez read the letter, reread parts of it, and then laid it down. He looked at them a little sadly.

'I regret to inform you that this house does not belong to your husband. This letter is dated November 26, but Mr Heywood had fallen behind on his payments to the property company long before that. The company repossessed the house at the end of October, so in November it was no longer Mr Heywood's to give your husband.'

'That can't be true! My husband wouldn't be deceived like that!'

But her daughter's heart was sinking as Señor Gomez continued.

'I can show you all the documents at the company's office. This house now belongs to them, and they have rented it to the Wilsons.' He looked round. 'I am sorry your husband has been deceived, and also that you have suffered a burglary, but I am afraid I must ask you to leave this house immediately so that work can start as soon as possible. I shall have to arrange repairs to the window, as well as the items you mentioned, before the Wilsons arrive. Then the house will have to be cleaned.'

'What?' Mrs Dale exploded. 'You can't throw us out! What happens if my husband comes here expecting to find us?'

Cara looked pleadingly at the agent.

'You have no right to be here,' Señor Gomez said sternly. Then his expression softened a little as he looked at their appalled faces. 'But it is not your fault, after all, and it is too late to arrange for any workmen today. You may stay here tonight, on condition you leave first thing in the morning. If you leave details of where you are going I will see

28

they are passed on to anyone who enquires.' He coughed. 'I am sure that, under the circumstances, the property company will not expect you to pay rent for the time you have spent here.'

In spite of their appeals, that was all he would concede. He left, making it clear that he would return in the morning to make sure that they had gone.

Left alone together, mother and daughter stared at each other hopelessly. Cara took a deep breath.

'I'll make us that cup of tea.'

When Cara came back with the tray, there were tears rolling down her mother's face.

'Don't worry.' Cara put the tray down so she could wrap her arms round her mother. 'We'll think of something. Father will see to it.'

But the sound of those words, repeated so often during her married life, upset her mother even more.

'Bob was so proud!' she sobbed. 'After all these years, we finally owned a house — even if it was in Spain. He was hoping we would all spend Christmas together here. Now what are we going to do?'

Cara handed her mother a cup.

'First of all, you start packing while I phone Malaga Airport and find out what flights back to England there are this evening or tomorrow. You'll have to contact Father, and tell him not to come.'

Mrs Dale was shaking her head.

'I don't know where he is! You know how he hates mobile phones, and refuses to have one. He said he'd call us when he had any news.'

Cara had a vision of her father arriving to find strangers in the house he'd thought was his. She couldn't warn Geoff not to come, since she'd never explicitly invited him.

'What can we do, instead of going back to England?'

Her mother sat up.

'We can stay at the hotel! Then if — when — your father arrives he can come and join us.'

'Suppose the hotel is full?'

'There's always an empty room somewhere.'

'It would be expensive over Christmas. Can we afford it?'

Her mother shrugged.

'It can go on my credit card.'

There seemed no alternative, and eventually Cara and Mrs Dale walked over to the hotel, where the receptionist greeted them with a smile.

'You are here for dinner again? You must like our food.'

Cara shook her head.

'Not just for dinner this time. There are problems with our house and we need a room for the next ten days or so. Have you a vacancy?'

The receptionist hesitated.

'I will have to check. We are very busy at this time of the year.'

They waited anxiously while she clicked on the computer, and saw her frown as she inspected the results. Finally she turned back to them.

'There is one room,' she said hesitantly. 'It is the only double we have, but it's not in the best position.'

'If that is all there is, we will take it,' Cara said firmly. 'Will you move us if a better room becomes available?'

'Of course,' the receptionist replied.

'We will bring our luggage over tomorrow morning.'

The receptionist pressed a button and a sheet of paper whizzed out of the printer.

'Here are our rates.'

Cara looked at the figures and gulped. Even a poor room in a good hotel was clearly expensive at this time of the year.

'How would you like to pay?' the receptionist continued.

'With my credit card.'

Mrs Dale handed her the piece of plastic and the girl noted down the details before handing it back, informing her that her card would be debited in one week.

'That will be fine.' Mrs Dale smiled

sweetly. 'It's nearly time for dinner, so we might as well stay now we are here. It won't take us long to pack after we have eaten.'

Grateful that at least they'd have somewhere to eat and a bed to sleep in for a week or so, the two women retired to the bar for a drink before their meal. Cara sank down into the comfortable chair, sipping her drink, and closed her eyes, only to open them again as a voice addressed them.

'Mrs Dale, Cara. Are you eating here tonight as well?'

It was Mrs Clarke, with Nick by her side carrying two glasses.

Mrs Dale beamed as the newcomers sat down opposite them.

'You know we told you yesterday that we were having trouble with a leaking roof? We decided that it would be too uncomfortable to live in the house while the workmen were doing the repairs, so we decided to come and stay here at the hotel till they are finished!'

Admiring her mother's quick thinking, Cara smiled at Nick.

'It means that we can join in all the festivities here.'

'What a good idea!' Mrs Clarke said. 'We attended a talk this morning and the two reps told us what is planned. It all sounds very enjoyable. Now you'll be able to come on the trips with us!'

'But we're not on your package holiday . . . ' Cara began, but the older women brushed this aside.

'Nonsense! I'm sure they'll welcome you if we say you are our friends.'

'Besides, Cara, these holiday reps are always glad to sell a few more seats on excursions.'

'Resign yourself to your fate,' Nick advised Clara. 'You are coming sightseeing with us, and I hope you are sharing our table tonight.'

Nick's presence would definitely add to the pleasures of Christmas, Cara decided. She raised her glass.

'Then here's a toast to a happy Christmas!'

For the rest of the evening she did her best to forget the problems which the day had brought, dancing with Nick while their mothers chatted. But back at the house reality could no longer be ignored. It didn't take long to pack her own belongings, then she helped her mother with her inordinate amount of luggage.

They had a late-night cup of tea in the kitchen. Mrs Dale looked round and sighed, looking wistful.

'It was nice while it lasted — thinking we had a place which belonged to us.' Her shoulders sagged. 'We're not getting any younger. The kind of life we've led has been exciting, like a big adventure, but now I've started worrying about the future.'

Cara hugged her mother, who leaned gratefully against her daughter. But then she suddenly sat up and smiled.

'It'll be all right. Your father will sort everything out. After all, an ordinary life would be too dull for us now!'

They were up early the next morning to finish packing and prepare to leave. Cara called a taxi and the driver was loading their bags into it when Mr Gomez appeared. He spoke to the driver, who stopped lifting bags in order to lean against his vehicle and light a cigarette. Then the agent came into the house.

'I thought I should check that everything is all right.'

'You mean you want to make sure that we're not taking anything with us that we shouldn't?'

He smiled at Cara but didn't reply before making a swift inspection of the rooms. When he'd finished he nodded at the driver, who started loading their luggage again.

Cara held out a piece of paper.

'We shall be at this hotel — at least for the next week.'

He nodded again and put the note in his pocket.

'I hope you enjoy Christmas there,'

he said politely, and then they were free to go.

When Cara went into the hotel to collect the key to their room, the first person she saw there was Nick, who was hovering by the Reception Desk.

'I was looking out for you. Can I help with your luggage?'

'I'd be grateful,' she told him. 'Our driver will bring some, but Mother brought an enormous amount of stuff.'

Their room was on the ground floor, and they had to negotiate several corridors and turnings before they found it.

'Here it is at last!' Cara opened the door and walked in.

'Oh, dear!'

It was clear why this had been the last room available. It was at the back of the hotel, dark and stuffy, and its view was limited to the roof of the kitchens and ended in a brick wall. They could hear the sound of the kitchen's extractor fans and smell of food cooking drifted in when Cara opened the window to let in some fresh air.

Nick looked round and grimaced.

'I'd offer to swap with you, but I've only a single room.'

She tried to smile.

'It doesn't matter. We'll only be sleeping here, after all, and the receptionist has promised to move us if a better room comes up.'

Her mother sat on the edge of one of the beds.

'Fortunately neither of us snores,' she commented. 'Let's get unpacked and then we can relax.'

For once, the weather had relented, and the sun was shining with enough warmth for Cara to lie by the pool on a sun bed. After a while Nick Clarke came out of the hotel and took the bed beside her. Mrs Dale, already at the centre of a group of new friends, waved at them.

'Your mother seems cheerful, in spite of the awful room,' he commented. 'Mine would still be screaming at the receptionist!'

'Mother's got used to making the best of things.'

Nick glanced sideways at her.

'The disruption in your house must be pretty terrible if you still prefer to move to that awful room.'

She tensed, and then forced herself to relax.

'I suspect Mother used the workmen as an excuse to move into the hotel for Christmas,' she replied lightly. 'No cooking, no cleaning . . . yours must be enjoying it as well.'

'This is the first Christmas since she was married that my mother hasn't spent at home,' Nick said heavily. 'She's always done the whole traditional thing — puddings and cakes made months in advance, an enormous turkey, the works.' He shrugged. 'Things change. Now, would you like a coffee?'

He swung his long legs off the sun bed and walked to the snack bar. Cara watched him, reflecting that he was well-built without being too muscular, and that he moved with confident ease.

He was an inch or two taller than Geoff, she guessed.

The thought of Geoff wiped away her smile. Was he even now on his way here to join her?

She had a picture of him arriving at the house to be met by workmen, and hoped that Señor Gomez had given them the name of the hotel.

3

Cara's mother had persuaded Mrs Clarke to go with her on a thorough exploration of all the amenities the hotel had to offer, from the gift shop to the beauty salon.

'We've both booked hair-dos tomorrow morning,' she said happily at dinner. 'We want to look good for Christmas.'

'Tomorrow morning?' Nick looked at his mother. 'But we're booked to go up into the Sierra Nevada!'

Her face fell.

'I thought there was something. But I do want to get my hair done.' She smiled triumphantly. 'Cara can go instead of me! You'd like to go, wouldn't you, dear?'

Cara blinked.

'What does it involve?'

'Oh, you go up in the mountains and

41

look at views,' Mrs Clarke said airily. 'I was only going because Nick wanted to.'

It would be nice to see something of the surrounding countryside.

But Nick was shaking his head.

'The seat's booked in your name, Mum.'

'They're not going to want to see her passport! Just tell them she's me — Mary Clarke.'

His face cleared.

'That's an idea. Well, Mary Clarke, will you come sightseeing with me?'

'I'd love to, if it's possible.'

'I'll have a word with the reps.'

The two travel reps who looked after the package holiday guests were easy to find. Eileen, sweet-faced and cuddly, and Margaret, elegant with dark eyes and long legs, saw no reason why Cara shouldn't come.

'After all, you've booked and paid for two seats. It doesn't really matter about the name.' Eileen turned to Cara. 'Just remember, if anyone wants Mrs Clarke, you answer to that name!'

Cara was grateful. She knew she could never have persuaded her mother to go on an excursion to look at landscapes which didn't have any shopping included.

The next morning, soon after breakfast, Cara was waiting with Nick and other guests as the coach arrived. Bright sun shone dazzlingly on the puddles, though mounting clouds on the horizon threatened more rain.

The guide ticked their names as they climbed aboard the coach.

'Nick Clarke,' she repeated as he showed her their tickets. She smiled at Cara. 'And this is Mrs Clarke, your wife?'

Cara blushed and nodded, taking her seat beside Nick. She could feel him shaking with quiet laughter, and dug an elbow in his ribs.

'Just remember we're married if we go anywhere else with this guide,' she muttered.

Secretly, she was a little flattered that

the guide had considered her young enough to be Nick's wife. At least she hadn't been thought old enough to be his mother!

Rain was forecast for later in the day, but the sun shone as first the drive took them through a series of identical tourist resorts, all with similar-looking hotels and blocks of apartments. Then the road began to climb, and soon they were in the foothills, then climbing higher still. The narrow road was carved out of the mountainside with a cliff on one side and a precipitous drop on the other. Finally, great mountainous vistas opened before them. They halted at various viewpoints so that they could appreciate the contrast between the sunlit valleys and the dark grey sky forming a backcloth over the sea, and the cameras were all clicking away busily.

The coach stopped for coffee in a small town in a fold of the mountains. After a call on her mobile phone the guide informed them regretfully that they wouldn't be able to visit their original destination, a town even higher up, since the heavy rain had caused a landslide which had closed the road. Almost as she spoke the heavens opened again and the torrential rain recommenced, so that, after some time spent sheltering in the various souvenir shops, they all returned gratefully to the coach to make their way down the mountain.

'Have you enjoyed it, in spite of the rain?' Nick enquired, and Cara nodded, her face glowing.

'It's beautiful! I'm so grateful your mother decided she'd rather have her hair done than come with you.'

'It's a pity you couldn't have your boyfriend with you instead of me. What was his name?'

'Geoff,' she told him.

'And what's the situation there exactly? Are you engaged, and planning to marry soon?'

Cara sought for the right words.

'We have an understanding.'

'What does that mean?'

'Well — for example — I might comment that I'd like to live in a certain area, and Geoff will either agree or say he'd prefer somewhere else. We don't actually say so, but we both know that we are discussing where we might live together.'

'But no definite commitment.'

'No.' She wasn't about to tell him how much she wished Geoff would make that commitment. 'How about you? Is there a girlfriend?'

He smiled.

'From time to time. The current one tells me where she would like to live, and exactly the type of house she wants, and I nod!'

'But no commitment?'

'No. Like you, no commitment.'

They went on to talk about work. Nick seemed to understand her worries over her banking career, and in return described the light engineering company he worked for.

'Most firms know exactly what they

want, and we follow their instructions, but quite often they have a problem and come to us for a solution. Then we have a chance to experiment, to design something new. It does give me real pleasure when we have an idea and it works.'

They chatted companionably as the coach edged its way downwards until, suddenly, the road seemed to soften under their wheels.

'The road's giving way!' one woman screamed in alarm, but a second later the coach was back on firm ground.

'Don't worry, we've passed that bit,' the guide soothed, with a fixed smile, and the passengers relaxed.

Cara realised that, in the general alarm, she'd turned to Nick and had buried her face against his shirt, and that his arms were still holding her tightly. She could feel the warmth of his body and his heart beating against her face. She sat up, embarrassed, but Nick didn't appear to notice.

'That was a nasty moment. The rain

has obviously weakened the road surface there. Fortunately we are nearly back at the main road.'

Cara was still trembling slightly, and he took her hand in his reassuringly.

'Don't worry. I'll keep you safe.'

It was as if she had always wanted to hear those words. What a pity they came from a man ten years her junior!

*   *   *

At the hotel they were greeted with good news.

'One couple have had to go home suddenly,' Mrs Dale told Cara. 'Their daughter has taken ill. Of course, I'm sorry for them, but it does mean that we can have their room.'

The new room was on the second floor and full of light, overlooking the pool. By craning your neck to the left you could just see the sea. By the time they had transferred everything to the new room the sun had returned, and they enjoyed a quiet hour on the balcony enjoying their new view before going downstairs for afternoon tea.

A taxi was just drawing away from the hotel. Its only passenger, a broad-shouldered young man with wavy, golden hair crowning high cheekbones and a straight nose, had shouldered his way through the front door carrying a suitcase, and was now looking round him as if searching for someone.

'Geoff!' Cara gasped, and then ran towards him. 'I'm so glad! I hoped you would come!'

He dropped his case and smiled, obviously enjoying the warmth of her welcome. Then his expression changed to a frown.

'I thought you wanted me to come here for Christmas to stay with you in your father's house. But when I got to that address some workmen told me that you had moved to this hotel.'

Cara sighed and shook her head.

'It's a long story, but at least you found us.'

'Where am I going to sleep?' Geoff

said a little peevishly.

'Can't you stay here?'

He stared at her.

'I thought I would be your guest. I didn't expect to have to pay to stay in a hotel!'

There was indignation in his voice, as if he suspected her of luring him there under false pretences, but just at that moment Cara's mother made herself heard.

'So you are Geoff? I'm so pleased to meet you at last. I'm Cara's mother. Now, you are our guest, Geoff. We will pay for your stay here.'

Mrs Dale's charm had its effect. Geoff did make a token attempt to reject the offer, but was easily persuaded to accept.

'There might not be room here,' Cara warned him, but the receptionist leaned forward.

'Yes, we have one room.'

'We'll order tea,' Mrs Dale announced. 'You can join us, Geoff, after you have booked in.'

She bustled Cara off to the lounge.

'I can see why you've fallen for him, Cara. He's the handsomest man I've seen for ages! Though he did seem rather upset when he thought he wasn't going to get a free holiday.'

'Don't judge him too quickly, Mother. He's come a long way to see me, and he doesn't like sudden changes of plan. But you didn't have to offer to pay for him to stay, when we're not quite sure how much we will have to pay for ourselves!'

'Either we will be able to pay the lot, or we won't be able to pay any of it,' her mother replied airily. 'There's no point in worrying just now.'

Cara still believed Geoff should have insisted on paying for himself. Since he worked in the same bank as she did, she knew roughly what he earned, and knew that he could have afforded it.

She and Mrs Dale had finished drinking their tea before he reappeared. He had changed from English winter clothes to more suitable, lighter wear, but he still did not look happy.

'My room is dreadful!' he complained. 'It's big, but it's dark. It looks out on the kitchen roof and it smells of food!'

Cara and Mrs Dale offered their sympathy and avoided each other's eyes, and Mrs Dale soon made an excuse and took herself tactfully off.

Cara put her cup down.

'Come and look at the beach. I've been wanting to walk along it.'

In summer the sands would have been packed with holidaymakers, but now they had it practically to themselves, and strolled along hand in hand. Of course, Geoff wanted to know why they were not at the house. Cara told him the same story as she had the Clarkes — that the house had needed repairs and it was easier to move out until they were completed.

He accepted the explanation.

'How long will the workmen be?' was all he asked.

'Well, with Christmas in a couple of

days, they probably won't finish till after the holidays.'

'That's a pity. I may have to go back before the New Year.'

Cara gave a secret sigh of relief. With luck, he wouldn't discover the truth till later, if at all.

They walked on along the smooth, golden sand, occasionally stopping to examine a shell or a pretty stone. This was how Cara had hoped it would be. Impulsively, she swung in front of him, flung her arms round his neck and kissed him.

He responded, holding her to him tightly.

'When do you expect your father?'

'I don't know. He may not even be able to get here to join us before the New Year.'

'A pity. He will want to be with your mother, and you could get a room of your own. That would be very convenient.'

She freed herself, laughing.

'I don't think I want all the other

guests gossiping about me, thank you!'

They lingered on the beach until the sun was setting and it was time to change for dinner.

Back at the hotel, her mother was obviously considering his possibilities as a future son-in-law.

'He's very well-mannered, as well as good-looking. Did you say he is doing well at the bank?'

'He's several grades above me, and is expected to rise even higher.'

'A banker with a future! Well, if the worst comes to the worst we can ask him for help. He won't want to see his girlfriend thrown out of the hotel.'

Cara dropped the dress she was holding, appalled.

'Don't even think of it! Geoff is very strict about money matters. He thinks not being able to pay your debts is almost a crime!'

'We'd better keep him away from your father, then!'

'Have you heard from him?'

Her mother shook her head.

'He won't contact me unless he has news — good or bad.' She smiled reminiscently. 'I remember once, we were on holiday at a very smart hotel when he heard that he'd lost nearly all his money. We couldn't pay the bill, so I walked out of the hotel wearing almost all my clothes in layers, and we hitched a ride home in a lorry!' She sighed. 'I don't think I could do that these days.'

'Was that the time I was forced to swop the posh boarding-school for a state comprehensive?'

'Probably.' Mrs Dale looked at her daughter thoughtfully. 'You know, I don't think you've ever enjoyed the thrill of living with your father's way of life in the way I have.'

'Some bits have been fun, and most of it has been exciting,' she commented, not wanting to upset her mother.

★ ★ ★

At dinner, the head waiter smiled welcomingly at Mrs Dale, who gestured to Geoff. 'As you see, a friend has joined us, Manuel. Can you find us a table for five, perhaps?'

For her, of course, it was possible.

'For five?' Geoff enquired. 'Who's joining us?'

'A friend of mine, Mrs Clarke, and her son, Nick. You two young men should get on very well.'

She couldn't have been more wrong. When the waiter showed the Clarkes to the new table Geoff stood up politely to greet them while Cara's mother introduced them. Mrs Clarke gazed admiringly at Geoff, but Cara could almost see ice forming in the air between him and Nick.

They were very different, of course. Geoff's classical good looks were unlike Nick's attractive but slightly irregular features.

While Nick had a ready, friendly smile, Geoff could seem standoffish till you got to know him.

Their careers were very different too.

'I work in a bank,' Geoff said a little

smugly in response to the obvious question. 'And you?'

'In a tool-making factory.' The answer came in the politest of tones.

'You make things?' Geoff said patronisingly. 'You, personally?'

'Quite often,' Nick replied crisply. 'It's one way of making sure it works.'

'A hands-on man.'

'Don't you actually count the money in a bank?'

'The counter staff do. I move large amounts about electronically, but I don't actually deal with any physically.'

'In fact, you just stare at a computer screen all day.'

That was enough, Cara thought, interrupting.

'Did you go to Nerja this afternoon?' Mrs Clarke's face lit up.

'We did indeed. It's a lovely town. We walked along, looking out to sea, and then explored lots of narrow streets with all kinds of shops.'

The conversation was safely diverted

to shopping and the best souvenirs to take home.

After the meal the small party moved into the lounge for coffee. Geoff lingered behind, holding Cara back.

'Do we have to spend any more time with that couple? I don't like the son. He's not our age or our type.'

'Nick? He's nice, and my mother likes his.'

Geoff gave an undignified snort.

'That's another thing! Isn't he a bit old to go on holiday with his mother?'

'That's mean, Geoff! She lost her husband earlier this year, and he was afraid she would be lonely.'

'Well, I still don't want to sit talking to him all evening. Can't we go for another walk?'

Cara sighed heavily.

'Look out of the window, Geoff. The rain is back.'

The rest of the evening was spent by the group making polite conversation until Mrs Dale happened to remark that it would be Christmas Eve the following day.

'It will seem odd to be here, instead of fighting our way through the crowds in the shops, buying last-minute presents.'

Mrs Clarke's lips quivered.

'I always spent Christmas Eve baking mince pies and decorating the Christmas tree.'

Tears filled her eyes, but Mrs Dale was instantly beside her, holding her comfortingly and offering her a tissue.

'I'm sorry,' the widow apologised, 'but it is going to be difficult to forget all the other times, even here.'

Soon afterwards, by mutual consent, they all decided on an early night.

'I still have to finish unpacking,' Geoff commented. 'I just hope the smells from the kitchen have stopped now that dinner is finished. At least, now it's dark, I won't be able to see the awful view.' His voice was scathing.

Nick's eyes lit up and he grinned at Cara, who shook her head warningly.

Back in their bedroom once again, Mrs Dale said how sorry she felt for Mrs Clarke. Clearly she was considering herself fortunate in comparison.

'You can see she is still grieving.'

'Yes,' Cara said thoughtfully. 'Nick's hoping that the different surroundings will help, of course.' She looked at her mother enquiringly. 'Has she told you what happened to him?'

Mrs Dale shook her head.

'I don't like to ask, and she hasn't volunteered any information so far.' She looked at Cara. 'Your young men don't like each other much, do they?'

'They are not 'mine', thank you very much. Nick is very nice, but Geoff is my boyfriend.'

'Yes. He has come all the way to Spain to spend Christmas with you. He must care for you. Has he said so?'

'Not in so many words, but we have an understanding.'

Mrs Dale sniffed derisively.

'I still believe in a proper proposal and a ring on your finger. Then you know where you are.'

'We live in modern times,' Cara responded with dignity.

Later, curled up in bed, she admitted to herself that she did want desperately to hear Geoff say he loved her and wanted to spend the rest of his life with her. There had been other relationships in her life, but until Geoff appeared Cara had never met anyone she wanted to share the rest of her life with. One rejected suitor had told her bitterly that she was looking for perfection but would never find it.

She knew that what she wanted was security. To be financially and emotionally secure, to know that there would always be a steady income to pay the bills. She did not want surprises.

4

Cara woke up excited and expectant, and it took her a minute or two to realise why. It was Christmas Eve! Here in Spain she'd escaped the shopping, cooking and list-making that marked the lead-up to the festival in England. Apparently the Spaniards made this a day to rejoice, not a twelve-hour, panic-driven endurance test of buying and baking!

As her mother stirred lazily, Cara opened the curtains and was greeted by a brilliantly blue sky.

'What shall we do today?'

Her mother groaned.

'Oh, dear, you sound in one of your active moods. Can I have breakfast before I decide?'

Suitably fed and given enough coffee, however, even Mrs Dale could be persuaded that it was a special day.

'Let's see how the Spaniards celebrate,' Cara suggested. 'We can walk into Nerja and see what's going on.'

It was a pleasant stroll along the seafront, and then they spent an enjoyable couple of hours looking at the decorations and peeping into churches that seemed as full of colour and bustle as the shops.

Finally, inevitably, it was coffee time. Cara rummaged in her jacket pockets but could only find a couple of coins. Fortunately her mother had brought her handbag.

'I'm nearly out of cash as well, but I've got my card here. I'll get some from the cash machine.'

They found a bank with a machine outside it and Mrs Dale inserted her card and punched the appropriate keys. Nothing happened. She tried again, then frowned at the screen and bit her lip before pressing the button that returned her card.

'It won't accept it, I'm afraid.'

'Let's try another cash machine,'

Cara suggested, but her mother shook her head.

'It said there were insufficient funds,' she said reluctantly, looking soberly at Cara. 'It means there isn't any money in the bank account. We're broke.' She gave her daughter a wry grin. 'Don't look so horrified. I've been here before, and it's not the end of the world.'

'But we were going to pay the hotel bill with your card!'

'Today's the twenty-fourth. The hotel doesn't want paying till the twenty-eighth. By then your father will have paid something in.'

'Supposing he doesn't? Supposing he *can't*?' Cara wailed, panicked.

'We'll worry about that in four days' time. Meanwhile, don't worry.'

Cara was no longer aware of the spectacular seascape as they walked rather wearily back to the hotel. She glanced at her mother and saw her walking with head bent, frowning. The woman was obviously less optimistic than she tried to appear.

She felt a spurt of anger at her father. Didn't he realise that his wife, and he himself, had reached an age when insecurity was too much of a strain? Her own credit card had a low limit, not enough to pay the hotel bill, and because of the cost of setting up her house there was virtually nothing in her bank account. All she could do was hope that her father would indeed perform one of his financial miracles, because otherwise she'd no idea what they could do. Once back at the hotel, in spite of her mother's reluctance she insisted they talk about the problem.

'What can we say to the hotel if no more money arrives?'

'We say there's been a misunderstanding, and that it's only a matter of time before we can pay the bill.'

'How long will they wait? At least Geoff can pay his own bill if necessary, though I doubt if he will ever forgive me. I think I can afford a couple of cheap flights back to England — if the hotel will let us leave the country. You'll have to go home and wait for Father to appear there.'

Her mother shifted uneasily.

'The problem there is — I haven't a home to go to. There was some unpleasantness with the landlord of our flat . . . '

'You mean you didn't pay the rent?' Cara interrupted.

'We'd have done so eventually — we always do, in the end — but the man was most unreasonable. Anyway, when your father was offered this house in Spain, it seemed a marvellous answer to our problems. It was somewhere I could live for a while, and in the meantime he'd sort things out.' She looked at her daughter pleadingly. 'I've always wanted to give you things, to help you. This house was a place for me to stay, and it also meant that I could give you a holiday in Spain. I was so happy, but then it all went wrong!'

She looked about to burst into tears, and Cara embraced her.

'It was a lovely idea. Let's wait and

see what happens. You can always stay with me in my place for a while.'

'The two of us in your small house?' Her mother raised a watery smile. 'We'd be screaming at each other in a week. You'd expect me to cook, and do housework!'

Cara glanced at her watch.

'Time to forget our problems — it's lunchtime. Let's eat while we can.'

She ate more than usual for lunch.

'Your walk has worked up a good appetite,' Geoff commented.

She smiled, wondering secretly if she was eating so much because she was afraid that, in four days' time, the supply of meals might stop abruptly!

After lunch the five of them formed a small group in the lounge, which was now covered with Christmas decorations.

'I must say, the hotel has made an effort,' Mrs Clarke said grudgingly. 'But we always bought a fresh tree.'

'We had the same decorations year after year,' Nick joined in. 'There was one small Father Christmas . . . '

He never finished the sentence. Instead, he was staring disbelievingly at the door. Cara turned and saw a girl just entering the lounge. She was tall and very slender, with straight black hair cut just below her ears. Cara couldn't decide whether the knitted garment she wore over black tights could be described as a jumper or a dress. It certainly showed most of her excellent legs. Every man, not only Nick, was looking at her.

'Lily!' Nick said in disbelief.

The newcomer saw him, gave a brilliant smile, and ran towards him, throwing herself into his arms.

Mrs Clarke was looking affronted.

'I don't know who she is. Nick didn't tell me he was expecting anyone.'

Lily had taken Nick's hand and he was leading her back to their table.

'Mother, may I introduce Lily, Lily Heyes.'

Lily smiled brilliantly and seized Mrs Clarke's reluctant hands.

'So you are Nick's mother! I'm so glad to meet you at last. Nick is always saying how wonderful you are. You look marvellous! The sun must suit you.'

Mrs Clarke melted instantly under this flattering onslaught and was soon welcoming Lily to the group.

'Nick didn't tell me you were coming, Lily.'

'I didn't know.' Nick said a little flatly.

Lily flung back her head and laughed.

'Of course you didn't! I didn't know myself till yesterday. I was all set to spend a traditional Christmas in England, and then I decided I had to be with you. So here I am!'

'Can I get you a coffee?' Geoff asked eagerly.

Lily turned the gaze of her large black eyes on him and Cara, torn between amusement and annoyance, saw him blush like a schoolboy.

'I'd love some.'

She sank down into an armchair, an

action which raised the hemline of her garment even higher.

Geoff rushed off while Mrs Clarke introduced the Dales.

'The poor things were supposed to be spending Christmas at their house near here,' she explained, 'but now it's full of workmen.'

Lily made sympathetic noises, but then turned again to Mrs Clarke.

'And how are you coping with this Christmas — without your husband and far away from home?'

Mrs Clarke, who minutes before had seemed to have been enjoying herself, heaved a deep sigh and cast her eyes downwards.

'I am managing somehow — for Nick's sake.'

Nick leaned forward.

'Are you staying here in this hotel, Lily?'

'Of course.'

'Where's your room?'

'On the third floor. I am lucky, I have a great view of the sea.' She smiled.

* * *

Soon afterwards, the little group broke up. Dinner on Christmas Eve was to be the main festive meal. The reps had warned them that it would go on for some time, and had advised a siesta that afternoon.

Mrs Dale, long used to financial crises, slept soundly, but Cara tossed and turned, worried about the moment they would be presented with a large hotel bill. Finally, she gave up trying to sleep. She let herself out of the room and made her way downstairs, then headed for the beach. It seemed deserted, and she wandered along the water's edge, soothed by the murmur of the sea. Then she saw someone sitting on a rock, throwing pebbles into the water. He looked up, and she recognised Nick.

'Didn't you feel like a siesta either?'
She sank down near him.
'I wanted fresh air and a chance to think.'

'Same here.' He threw another pebble. 'Cara, your friend Geoff had trouble getting a room here when he arrived without booking, and he ended up in that awful room you were given at first.'

She nodded.

'Yet Lily arrives out of the blue today, and is given one of the best rooms in the hotel.' He threw another stone viciously. 'It looks as if she planned to come here all the time. She must have booked well in advance.'

'Isn't that a compliment?' Cara suggested. 'She wanted to be sure she could spend Christmas with you.'

'But why pretend she came on impulse? I don't like being deceived. And I wanted to be able to concentrate on Mum this Christmas, to make sure she was happy.' He sighed, and turned to her. 'Lily is great fun as a girlfriend, but at the moment that's all she is to me. She's trying too hard to make me feel that we are a couple. I don't like the pressure, but it's going to be hard letting her down, especially when she's clearly aiming to get my mother on her side.'

Another stone splashed in the water.

'I'm sorry. You said you needed a chance to think. Have you got a problem as well?'

Cara was tempted to tell him everything, to ask his advice, but she suppressed the urge. She knew from experience how people could grow cool and withdrawn when you talked about money problems, perhaps fearing you were about to ask them for a loan.

So she smiled, and said it was just a decision she had to make.

Nick gave her a sideways look.

'Well, he's good-looking, he has a good job and prospects. He's not perfect, but you could do worse.'

'Thank you for the agony aunt advice, based on all your years of experience,' she replied tartly. 'I'll think about it.'

He ruffled his hair with one hand and grinned.

'Sorry. I was just being practical. Well, we both seem to have romantic problems. Let's go back to the hotel for a drink.'

Cara found it comforting to stroll along beside him, chatting idly. Back at the hotel, everyone was clearly dressing up for the occasion.

Mrs Dale had chosen an elegant silk top with floor-length skirt, a souvenir from one of her affluent periods. No longer in the latest style, its quality showed it had come from a very prestigious designer. Around her neck, of course, she wore her gold chain. Cara's packing had included one long, floaty dress which her mother said showed off her figure beautifully, and she was pleased with what she saw in the mirror. She checked her lipstick and patted her hair.

The hotel guests began to assemble in the bar and reception area well before the meal was due to start, and there was a steady buzz of anticipation. For most of the women this was the only occasion apart from New Year's Eve when they'd have an opportunity to wear their full-length dresses. A few of the men were in dinner jackets. Geoff greeted Cara and Mrs Dale with warm compliments which Nick echoed, then there was a sudden hush and all heads turned to the doorway as Lily made her entrance. She was still in black tights, though now of sheer silk, and above them she wore a crimson silk tunic which slipped down over one bare shoulder. Her black hair, dramatically outlined eyes and crimson lips complemented her costume, and for a moment all the women found themselves ignored.

'Doesn't she look marvellous?' Mrs Clarke cried.

Whatever Nick thought of Lily's planned arrival, he now claimed his girlfriend eagerly, and Geoff was full of effusive praise.

'You make everybody else look dull,' he told her, before becoming aware of the eyes of both Cara and Mrs Dale boring into him. 'Except for you, of course, darling,' he said hastily but too late.

Lily took the compliments as her due before admiring Mrs Dale and Mrs Clarke's outfits. Then she turned to Cara and inspected her slowly.

'That is a lovely dress, Cara. It's very like one my mother used to have, but then you and she are pretty near in age, I suppose.'

Cara pressed her lips shut. In a few days neither she nor, presumably, Geoff would ever see Lily again. She could put up with her for that time, couldn't she?

But she wondered why Lily felt so antagonistic towards her. Surely she wasn't jealous of Cara's friendship with Nick?

The waiters began to move among the guests, offering them glasses of sparkling Spanish wine. Then the restaurant doors opened and the head waiter stood ready to receive the hungry diners.

The little group was ushered to its table where Cara picked up the menu. Her eyes widened.

'Have you seen this?' she demanded. 'Six courses — I can't possibly eat so much!'

It was a superb meal, from the fish soup to the spheres of chocolate served with brandy butter, but most people, like Cara, found their appetite flagging long before the end. Geoff, she noticed, managed to clear his plate of every course and so, interestingly, did Lily.

There was dancing afterwards for those still able to move. Cara found herself dancing with Nick but they said little. Perhaps because they were both aware of the other couple, Geoff and Lily, dancing close together and obviously enjoying each other's company just a little too much.

As midnight approached and the mothers decided it was bedtime for them, Nick suggested a retreat out on to the balcony for some fresh air. Stars shone in the clear black sky, and the recent rain had brought out the smell of grass from the hills. It was just possible to hear the waves breaking gently on the sand.

'No wonder the English love Spain in winter,' Cara exclaimed.

Geoff shook his head.

'It doesn't seem right. Christmas should have fir trees and snow.'

'That's the traditional view. But in fact, as far as I can remember, it's usually raining, and everyone buys plastic trees because they don't shed needles on the carpet!'

'How cynical, Nick. I thought your family always had a very traditional Christmas.' Cara hesitated. 'How is your mother feeling, since this is her first Christmas without your father.'

There was a delay before Nick replied.

'Better than she expected, as far as I can make out.' He glanced at his wrist. 'Ten seconds to Christmas Day. Let's count them down.'

'Ten, nine, eight, seven, six, five, four,

three, two, one!' they chorused.

'Happy Christmas, darling!' Geoff kissed Cara soundly.

'Happy Christmas, Nick!' Lily echoed, grabbing him tight as she spoke. For a few seconds, all was right with the world.

5

The clock said nine o'clock when Cara woke on Christmas Day. She lay still for a few minutes, remembering other Christmases with her parents, ranging from the luxurious to the hastily improvised. There had always been presents for her, however, and much laughter and love. She looked across at her mother's bed and saw that Mrs Dale was already awake.

'Happy Christmas, Mother!' she said softly, and her mother blew her a kiss before bending over and rummaging under her bed, emerging with a parcel wrapped untidily in red paper. She tossed it to Cara.

'Happy Christmas, darling!'

It was a pure silk scarf in brilliant scarlet. Cara exclaimed in delight while her mother watched anxiously.

'It's not much, I know . . . '

'It's beautiful!' Cara draped it round her neck while she looked in the mirror. 'It suits my colouring perfectly, and it's so soft.'

She opened her own suitcase and took out a small package.

'Here's your present.'

It was a small antique brooch in turquoise and silver.

'I got it because I know turquoise is your birthstone, and because it's pretty — like you,' Cara told her.

'It's a lovely present.' Her mother had tears in her eyes. 'I know your father and I haven't been the best of parents, but we have managed to produce a wonderful daughter.

The two embraced and Cara sniffed.

'We'll have to stop this! It's Christmas Day and we can't go down to breakfast red-eyed!'

'I do feel a bit weepy. It's the first Christmas I've spent without your father since we were married.' She grasped Cara's sleeve. 'That reminds me. We'll have to be very nice to Mrs

Clarke and try to cheer her up if she gets upset.'

At first glance, everybody at breakfast was very happy, greeted at the restaurant door with glasses of Buck's Fizz. Nick sat alone at their table and insisted on giving both of them a Christmas kiss.

He held Cara a moment longer than he had her mother, smiling down into her eyes. 'Happy Christmas, happy holiday, happy future.'

Cara repeated his words, feeling more light-hearted than she had for the past few days. She was enjoying herself, in a comfortable hotel, and Geoff was here as well. Her father had surely solved the money problem by now. There was nothing to worry about.

Even Lily's appearance in her favourite black and scarlet, with miniature Santas swinging from each ear, could not spoil her mood. After breakfast she sat in a quiet corner of the lounge, where Geoff found her and greeted her with a warm kiss before offering a package.

'I overslept, the result of that dinner last night,' he apologised. 'Happy Christmas, and I hope you like this. Open it!'

It was a bottle of a well-known perfume.

She smiled and embraced him, keeping quiet about the fact that she had seen that particular brand on special offer at the Duty Free in England. Then she gave him her present — a pair of slim gold cuff-links which had cost her more than she could really afford.

'Fourteen carat. Good quality,' he said appreciatively.

By mid-morning all presents had been delivered, though Lily explained that, because of her last-minute decision to come to Spain, she had not had time to buy any.

'But then, nobody has given me any either,' she pointed out, pouting.

'I have one for you back in England.'

Nick spoke defensively.

He was rewarded with a brilliant smile.

'Then I shall look forward to it.' She lowered her voice and whispered intimately in his ear. He reddened and looked round in embarrassment.

Suddenly Margaret and Eileen, the two travel reps, erupted into the middle of the guests. They were wearing Santa Claus hats and — more surprisingly — Wellington boots.

'Come on, everybody!' Eileen said. 'It's Christmas morning, and you've all to come paddle in the sea!'

Some guests groaned and sank deeper into their chairs, but a fair number followed Margaret and Eileen through the gardens and across the beach. Once there, the reps bravely took off their boots and waded barefoot into the sea. 'Come on!' they shouted. 'It's lovely once you're in!'

First one brave soul, then another, then another, took off their shoes and ventured into the water.

'Come on, Geoff. We have to go in!' Cara sat down on the beach and took off her shoes.

'Not my type of thing,' he replied. 'I think it's rather silly.'

Ignoring him, she ran into the sea. Soon she was happily stamping and splashing in the water. She felt like a child again on a first exhilarating visit to the seaside. The brave paddlers took each other's hands and formed a circle, making up an impromptu dance that left them very wet. Cara realised that she was holding Nick's hand.

Back on the beach, Geoff and Lily received their soaked partners with disapproving faces.

'You'd better change at once, Cara, before you catch a cold,' was Geoff's comment.

Mindful of its English guests, the hotel provided a full traditional Christmas lunch, the second enormous meal in twenty-four hours. Afterwards, the hotel fell quiet as most guests retreated to their rooms or the sunbeds to sleep off their over-indulgence. The Dales and the Clarkes settled by the swimming-pool.

'I must admit that it's very pleasant to have your meal served to you without having to bother with any cooking or washing-up.'

Nick grinned conspiratorially at Cara over his mother's head.

'Success!' he mouthed.

Cara's eyes closed and she relaxed, deliberately emptying her mind of all thoughts, enjoying the warmth of the sun. She slept.

*   *   *

She was woken abruptly by a scream. She jerked upright, looking wildly around the roof.

Mrs Clarke was shouting angrily at a man who stood in front of her, while at the same time she seemed to be trying to wave him away. The man, who looked about sixty, was trying to speak to her but she would not listen.

'Go away! I never want to see you again!'

'But, Mary . . . '

'Go away! Haven't you humiliated me enough? If you don't go at once, I'll call the hotel staff and have you thrown out!'

She took a deep breath threateningly, and the man gave in.

'I'm going,' he said hastily, then turned to Nick, who was staring at him in amazement. 'Nick, can I talk to you?'

Nick swung his long legs off his sunbed, stood up and led the stranger away. Mrs Clarke promptly collapsed in hysterical tears and Mrs Dale hurried to take her in her arms.

'There, dear.' She cuddled the weeping woman like a child, shielding her from the stares of other sunbathers.

'Everything is all right now. The nasty man has gone. Whoever he was,' she added, agog with curiosity.

'It was Andrew,' Mrs Clarke wailed.

'Who's Andrew?'

'My husband — Nick's father!'

Cara and her mother looked at each other in silence.

'But I thought your husband was dead. You said you'd lost him.'

'I did lose him. He left me six months ago!'

Mrs Dale's mouth opened, then shut firmly as she looked around at the eager audience.

'Come along now, dear. This place is much too crowded. Let's take you to your room.'

Between them, Cara and her mother supported Mrs Clarke to the lift and then to her room.

'I'll see you later,' Mrs Dale murmured to Cara, who nodded and went back to the pool to gather up their belongings. There was no sign of Nick, and she decided she might as well sit down again and await further developments by the pool.

Soon afterwards, Geoff appeared, still sleepy-eyed. He found a waiter and ordered tea for two, then went back to change the order to three when Lily appeared.

'Where's everybody else?'

'Something upset Mrs Clarke,' Cara replied. 'My mother is looking after her at present.'

'What upset her?'

'Her husband.'

'But he's dead!'

Cara shook her head.

'Apparently not. I woke up and he was standing in front of Mrs Clarke. She screamed at him and then Nick took him away. That's all I know.'

'I must find Nick. He may need me,' Lily stated, and when Geoff returned with the tea-tray only Cara was there.

Very briefly she explained what had happened.

'But she said her husband was dead.'

'No. She never actually said that. She always said that he was gone, or that she had lost him.'

At this moment Lily returned, looking displeased.

'I can't find Nick, and your mother

won't let me see Mrs Clarke,' she complained petulantly.

'Presumably we'll learn all about it eventually,' Cara said soothingly.

'But I want to know now!' Lily said. 'It might affect me.'

Cara finished her tea and excused herself, saying she'd had enough sun. Taking a roundabout route, she went to the spot on the beach where she and Nick had met before.

She'd guessed right. He was sitting on the same rock, grim-faced.

He looked up as he heard her footsteps on the pebbles and nodded a light greeting.

'What's happening back at the hotel?'

'My mother is looking after your mother, Lily wants to know what is going on, and Geoff is looking after her.'

Nick almost managed a smile.

'Well, that scene by the pool added excitement to a dull afternoon.'

Cara sat down on the beach.

'Well?' she said finally. 'Aren't you

going to start throwing stones?'

He gave a short, surprised bark of laughter.

'That wouldn't be enough today.' He looked at her ruefully. 'I suppose you want to hear all about it.'

'Of course! Was that your father? Where is he now?'

He gazed out to sea.

'That was my father, and he's gone back to his hotel in Nerja.' There was a pause, and then his words came tumbling out. 'He left my mother after twenty-eight years of marriage. He was offered early retirement last January, took it, then just mooched around the house, doing nothing. I think he felt there was no purpose left to his life. I moved out into my own flat, and one day he announced that, now I was gone, there was nothing to keep him there. He was bored and had been for years, and he wanted a new, more fulfilling life. So he walked out, though he left Mum with the house and most of the money.'

'Didn't your mother know he was unhappy?'

Nick shook his head.

'She was always busy with committees and other activities. I think she assumed he'd take up golf or something.'

'And was there someone else?'

'You mean had he fallen for some girl who made him feel young again? No. I think Mum would have felt a bit better if there had been! After all, to be told that your husband can't bear to stay with you any longer because you are so boring is humiliating.'

'She must have been very upset.'

'She was angry. At one time she blamed me. Apparently, if I hadn't left home and disrupted the way we lived, my father would never have left.'

For a moment Nick looked like a teenager who has been wrongly accused of some fault by his parents. Cara subdued an impulse to imitate her mother and give him a comforting hug.

'So what went wrong? Why did he

appear today without any warning?'

Nick bit his lip.

'I don't know the whole story, but I think he found that trying to start a new life on your own at sixty was a lot more difficult than he thought it would be. He went on a couple of holidays and felt lonely, because everybody else had a partner. He was just as bored as he had been at home, except now he had to cope with his dirty clothes and feed himself. He hadn't thought about things like that. I suspect he would have liked to come back to Mum months ago, but he felt he'd made a fool of himself and couldn't admit it.

'So he decided to make a dramatic return at Christmas, expecting to be welcomed with open arms. An old friend told him where we'd be, and he rolled up here this afternoon — as you saw.'

'That's very sad. Now you've got two unhappy parents.'

He kicked a rock viciously.

'Ow!' Even inanimate objects were out to get him.

He rubbed his toe furiously, and looked up at Cara in almost despair.

'What can I do?'

'It's their problem, not yours.'

'I suppose you're right, but I'll have to try and help.'

She hesitated, searching for some way she could give Nick comfort.

'What are you going to do now?'

'I think I'll go for a walk along the beach to try and clear my mind.'

His unhappy expression was too much. Cara found herself on her knees beside him, her arms round his shoulders. He turned, lifted his hand, and gently drew one finger down her face from brow to chin. She shivered at his touch. Their faces were inches apart as they looked into each other's eyes. For a second neither moved, then Cara drew herself away sharply and gave an uneasy laugh.

He stood up, staring at his feet and then the sea, anywhere but at her.

'Thanks for listening.'

'But that wasn't all she was doing, was it?' an angry voice said.

They swung round and saw Geoff standing a few feet away, glaring at them. Cara moved swiftly towards him.

'Geoff, I was just being sympathetic!'

Geoff ignored her and strode forward till he was face to face with Nick.

'Isn't Lily enough for you? Are you trying to steal my girlfriend as well?'

'Don't talk nonsense. Cara's telling you the truth, she was being kind.'

'I've seen the way you've been looking at her . . . '

Cara was torn between two emotions — amazement that, for the first time in her life, two men were quarrelling over her — and sheer fury because the two of them were being so stupid.

'Stop this at once! Nick is upset because he's got a major problem. I put my arms round him to comfort him, Geoff. He's ten years younger than I am, for heaven's sake!'

The two men glared for a few more

seconds, then the tension eased.

'I'm sorry,' Geoff mumbled. 'But I care for you, Cara, and when I saw you with your arms round another man it made me angry.'

'There was no need. You heard what she said. To her I'm just a boy.'

Cara watched him walk away.

'I'm sorry,' Geoff said again. 'I was jealous.'

'You made a fool of yourself,' she snapped. 'Let's get back to the hotel and forget this little scene.'

★　★　★

Mrs Dale was in their room, lying on her bed exhausted.

'She cried herself to sleep finally. What a silly man, turning up like that! He should have written to her, or phoned first. Have you found out anything?'

Cara told her what she had learned from Nick and Mrs Dale groaned.

'So life without his wife was as boring

as life with her! Maybe the fault was in him, then. Well, if someone had left me and then turned up expecting a big welcome, I'd have hit them and pushed them in the pool! But Nick shouldn't feel guilty. Children have a right to their own lives.' She yawned. 'I need to catch up with my siesta.'

Her eyes closed, then reopened.

'Does Lily know what has happened?'

'She knows Nick's father has appeared, that's all.'

'Well, I hope she doesn't disturb Mary Clarke. The poor woman needs some quiet time.'

Her eyes closed, and soon her regular breathing showed that she had fallen asleep.

Cara found it difficult to settle. It seemed that almost every day somebody new appeared — first Geoff, then Lily, and now Mr Clarke. Why couldn't it be her own father who walked through the door?

She sighed, pummelling her pillow.

Her dream of a quiet romantic Christmas break with Geoff was gone, so she was going to forget everybody else's problems and concentrate on him. His anger when he found her with Nick had shown he cared for her, after all.

With that in mind, she dressed carefully for dinner and took care to apply some of the perfume he had given her. She saw her mother watching her.

'I have to show I appreciate his gift,' she pointed out.

Mrs Dale only smiled.

Their dinner table was half-empty that night. There was no sign of Nick. Soon Lily came in, and made a great fuss about choosing a trayful of food to be taken up to Mrs Clarke.

'Mrs Clarke and I are eating in her room,' she informed them. 'I'm staying with her to look after her and comfort her.'

'When I left her all she needed was rest and time to think,' Mrs Dale said sharply, and was rewarded with a pitying smile.

'Is Nick with her?' Cara asked.

Lily's smooth assurance faltered.

'No. He hasn't been to see his mother or me. I don't know where he is.'

Mrs Dale stared balefully after Lily as she left the restaurant with the loaded tray.

'There are very few people I really dislike,' she said, 'but that girl is one of them. I pity Nick.'

'I think he can look after himself,' Cara murmured, then forgot Lily as Geoff appeared.

He looked at her sheepishly, but she had decided to be forgiving and greeted him with a smile as he sat beside her.

'I think it's just the three of us this evening. The Clarkes apparently don't feel like facing the world, understandably. So Lily is looking after Mrs Clarke, and Nick has vanished.'

'I can understand how they feel. I've just been in the bar, and everybody seems to know what happened by the pool. Still, it's nice to have the two of you to myself.'

It was a quiet evening. With many of the hotel staff taking a rest at home, entertainment consisted of a pianist playing dance tunes in the lounge. Geoff led Cara on to the small dance floor for a waltz.

'I know this isn't what we planned,' she said softly, 'but you are enjoying yourself, aren't you?'

'Of course,' he retorted. 'I'm with you, and being treated to a stay in a very comfortable hotel.'

Cara tried not to imagine how he would feel if her father didn't solve the financial problems and Geoff found out that Mrs Dale could not pay his hotel bill. She shivered, and he held her closer.

He bent his head and kissed her hair and she nestled in his arms. She was certain he loved her. If there was a crisis, surely he would help.

6

As always, December 26 was a bit of a let-down. The Christmas celebrations were over, but the days had to be filled somehow before New Year's Eve brought the holiday season to an end and signalled a return to normal life.

Lily and Mrs Dale seemed to be competing to see who could offer the most sympathy and support to Mrs Clarke. Nick only appeared briefly, and when there was almost totally silent.

That left Cara free to spend most of the day with Geoff. They walked along the coast road in the morning and sat companionably reading in the lounge in the afternoon. Once again, Cara thought what a good lifetime pair they would make. Maybe by the end of this holiday he would see it, too. She told herself to stop building castles in the air and just enjoy each day as it came, but still she dreamed wistfully of a proposal of marriage on New Year's Eve.

Nick came into dinner late, and nobody asked him where he had been, though his mother did cast reproachful looks his way. Lily was looking after her, collecting her food from the buffet, hurrying to fulfil her slightest wish, treating her as if she were an invalid.

'Thank you, Lily. I don't know what I should do without you,' Mrs Clarke said when Lily performed some service.

'Don't worry,' Lily reassured her, and then smiled at Nick. 'I shall always be here to help you. Won't I, Nick?'

Cara nearly choked on a mouthful. Obviously Lily thought that her unexpected appearance at the hotel hadn't had the effect she'd hoped for. Now she was trying to manoeuvre Nick into agreeing in front of everybody that she would always be with him and his mother, a very public commitment.

Nick raised his head and gave Lily a long, cold look.

'Your future friendship with my mother is something for the two of you to decide. I won't be involved.' He stood up.

'Excuse me,' he said, and walked out of the dining room.

An ugly tide of red swept Lily's face and there was an awkward silence at the table, broken by Mrs Clarke.

'Ignore him, Lily. It's all my husband's fault. He's upset Nick so he can't think of anything else.'

Everybody began to talk of various subjects — the weather, the food, the news — anything to change the subject. After the meal was finished Lily and Mrs Clarke did not stay to have coffee in the lounge.

'Well, that was humiliating. I can almost feel sorry for the girl,' Mrs Dale murmured to Cara. 'She did ask for it, though. She was trying to trick him.'

Geoff was condemning Nick's behaviour.

'He was unforgivably rude, especially after the way that poor girl has looked after his mother. Serves him right if she decides to have nothing more to do with him.'

He looked round.

'There she is at the bar now, probably getting coffee to take upstairs. I'll just have a word with her.'

He bustled off before the other two could say anything, and returned ten minutes later.

'I helped her take the coffee up,' he explained. 'She was upset, though she tried to hide it. I told her that Nick Clarke didn't deserve her. I think I helped her feel better.'

He leaned back with a definite trace of smugness. Cara wondered if he would have been so sympathetic if Lily hadn't been such an attractive girl, and then told herself that she was being mean when he looked at her anxiously a minute later.

'You didn't mind me going off to help Lily, did you?'

'No,' she said warmly. 'It just shows what a nice nature you've got.'

Later, up in their bedroom, Mrs Dale speculated on what would happen in the future.

'Lily is going to have to think of something extra special if she is going to make Nick forgive that trick.'

'It depends how he feels about her,' Cara responded. 'If he loves her, he is probably kicking himself and trying to think how he can make it up to her. I suppose he could blame anxiety about his father.'

'I'm not sure he does care for her all that much. I know he's young, but he's mature enough not to let a good pair of legs blind him to what she is like as a person! Anyway, it's not our problem.'

'No.' Cara sighed. 'We've got our own problems. The hotel will want paying the day after tomorrow, and we still haven't heard from my father.'

Her mother fingered the gold chain at her neck.

'We'll manage. Now, have a good night's sleep.'

Cara decided to go swimming with her mother the next morning, and Geoff announced that he would go for another walk. The indoor pool was pleasantly warm, and the feel of the water pouring over her skin was immensely soothing.

Cara forgot her worries and luxuriated in the sensation.

Afterwards, still happy, she saw Nick coming towards her in an upstairs corridor as she carried her wet towel and costume back to her room. In spite of his dour face she greeted him cheerfully. He stopped, and managed a ghost of a smile.

'Is everything going well for you?'

She nodded, and then, moved by his obvious unhappiness, put a hand on his arm.

'Nick, I know you are having trouble with your parents as well as with Lily, but, believe me, it will all sort itself out. I'm older than you. I've had more experience with life . . . '

But he interrupted her, shaking himself free from her hand.

'I am a mature adult, not a schoolboy, so please don't speak to me as if I were. You may be older than I am, but I can assure you that I have also learnt from experience. I'd be grateful if you would leave me to deal with my own problems.'

He brushed past her, leaving her staring after him, her good mood ruined. Well, let him cope by himself! She took a few steps along the corridor towards her room, then turned as she heard hasty footsteps. It was Nick, looking very shame-faced.

'Forgive me,' he said. 'I was unforgivably rude.'

When she didn't reply, he went on.

'I was beginning to think I could deal with one situation, but two at the same time is a bit too much for me.'

Cara felt her annoyance vanishing.

'Do you want to talk about it again?' she asked hesitantly. 'Honestly, I will just listen, and won't try to give advice.'

'Do you know, I think I would like that.' He looked round. 'But where could we go? Somewhere where your Geoff won't see us.'

'We could go in here,' Cara answered, opening the door of her room. 'Mother is having coffee with a group of confirmed gossips, so she won't be back for some time.'

A quick glance confirmed that the maid had straightened the beds and the room was reasonably tidy. Cara persuaded Nick to take the only armchair and perched on the bed opposite him.

'Now, just talk at me,' she ordered.

He leaned forward, elbows on his knees, and was silent for a while. Then he took a deep breath.

'I'll start with Lily,' he announced. 'I met her a couple of months ago, and we've seen a lot of each other since.' He glanced at Cara, his eyes veiled by his lashes.

'She's attractive, of course, and I think I felt flattered that I'd been able to get a girlfriend like her. However, after a while, I realised that we hadn't much in common, and I was prepared to let the affair die out.

'But Lily wouldn't let things end. She started telephoning me, asking me out, and it was difficult to make excuses, so like a fool I let the affair drag on for far too long.

'I thought that, if I was here over Christmas and out of contact, things would cool down naturally and she might find someone else.' His lips tightened.

'When she asked me where we would be staying, I assumed I might get a Christmas card or even a phone call. I certainly didn't expect her to book herself in here!'

Tentatively Cara raised a hand.

'This is a question, not advice,' she said hastily. 'I don't want to hurt your feelings but, why is she chasing you so hard? She doesn't give the impression of being madly in love with you, so just why is she so determined to get you?'

'I'm not sure,' he said, avoiding her eyes.

She was sure he was hiding something, but there was no point in persisting if he was unwilling to be frank, so she went on.

'After the way you reacted yesterday, when Lily tried to force you to say publicly that the two of you had a future together, I should think you won't see much more of her, if she has any pride at all!'

Nick's voice was bitter.

'You underestimate her. She came looking for me last night, apologised for embarrassing me and swore she never meant to. I should have warned her that I never intended to see her again once we got back to England, but I didn't want to be brutal. I just told her to forget it, and never to do it again. When I went down to breakfast this morning she appeared seconds later, and was virtually cooing over me. I'm sure she was there waiting for me.'

There was another silence.

'And your parents?' Cara asked at last.

Nick gave a harsh laugh.

'The other problem. Yes. I'll admit Dad made a fool of himself, marching off to find a new life as if he were forty years younger, but Mum should probably have realised how bored and aimless he felt. Even I could see how fed up he was each time I went home.

'The thing is, they had grown so used to each other over the years, with their own things to occupy them, that they'd stopped talking to each other about their emotions and feelings.

'And, of course, Dad couldn't have done anything worse than that dramatic appearance on Christmas Day! He thought it would be romantic, you understand. He didn't realise she had given everyone the impression that he was dead, and that his appearance left her with an awful lot of questions to answer.

'Besides, it made her feel a complete fool. At the moment, he's mooning

111

about Nerja, hoping she'll wake up one morning and decide to take him back, but she won't even let me mention him to her. Lily's being a nuisance there as well. She keeps going on about how badly he treated Mum. I suspect she thinks Mum on her own will be easier to influence.'

Yet another silence, till Nick finally sat up and produced a genuine smile.

'Thank you, Cara.'

'I haven't done anything.'

'You've listened, and that's what I needed. It hasn't solved the problems but I do feel better. Now I'd better go and see how Mum is.'

He went to the door, Cara following, and opened it, but before he walked away he looked down at Cara, then bent and kissed her swiftly on the lips. She gazed up at him, taken aback, but it never occurred to her to move away or protest.

'That was just another way of saying 'thank you',' he murmured.

Some slight noise attracted their

attention. Lily was standing in the corridor, looking at both of them with blazing fury in her eyes. She turned on her heel and almost ran away from them.

'We should always make sure other people aren't watching us when we get close!' Cara said a little shakily. 'I suspect your problem with Lily may have been solved for you.'

'In that case, I am deeply grateful. I'll tell you what happens later.'

★ ★ ★

After he had gone Cara sank into the armchair, which was still warm from his body. She leaned back and it was as if he were holding her. That was nonsense, she told herself. She was years older than he was, and he'd probably kissed her in the same way as he would have kissed an aunt who had done him a kindness.

Still, she was amazed at the thought that cool, calm and collected Cara

Dale, who always behaved so properly, had been seen kissing a man as he left her bedroom. Then she jerked upright. Suppose Lily tried to cause trouble by telling people what she'd seen? Suppose she told Geoff?

Cara scrambled to her feet. She must find him and be the first to tell him what had happened, making a joke of it, so that Lily could not poison his mind against her.

She hurried down to the reception area and breathed a sigh of relief as she saw Geoff coming through the front doors.

'Geoff, I must speak to you!' she said hurriedly.

'And I want to speak to you.'

They went into the small card room, empty at this hour, and sat down facing each other across one of the tables.

'Listen, Geoff, if Lily starts talking about me . . . '

He interrupted without apology.

'Bother Lily. I want an explanation from you. I decided to take a walk up to your father's house to see how the workmen were getting on. I found it occupied by a family who had never heard of you or your family, and who claimed to have rented the house from some agency. What's going on, Cara? Tell me!'

He glared at her while she looked back at him in confusion.

'I suppose I should have told you.'

'Does your father own the house or not?'

'I'm afraid not.'

'But back home you said that you and your mother were going to stay at your father's house!'

'Well, we thought we were.' Gradually Cara explained the whole sorry mess to him. 'So you see, when you did come, it would have been very embarrassing to have to tell you how my father had been tricked, so we let you think we'd moved because of the workmen.'

'You deceived me.'

'We misled you.'

Now Geoff was frowning over something else.

'I thought your father was a successful businessman. Surely he had the man's title to the house checked before he accepted it? And where is your father, anyway? Wasn't he supposed to be here for Christmas?'

Cara smiled wryly. Now everything was about to come out, in a way it was a relief.

'My father is a successful businessman . . . sometimes. At other times he guesses wrong or someone misleads him, and then he struggles to survive. He hasn't appeared here so far, we believe, because he has hit a bad patch and is in real trouble.'

Now for the real bad news, as far as Geoff was concerned.

'In fact, at the moment Mother and I can't even pay our hotel bill. I'm afraid you may have to pay for yourself.'

Geoff stared at her in horror, so she closed her eyes and ploughed on.

'In fact, I'd be most grateful if you

would lend us enough to pay our bill. I'll be able to pay you back in a few weeks.'

She finished in a rush and waited for his reaction.

There was total silence before Geoff replied, his voice almost trembling with emotion.

'Let's get this straight. I thought you were the daughter of a wealthy man. Now you tell me that he's a chancer — almost a gambler — who never knows from one day to another whether he'll be rich or penniless. Then you invited me to spend Christmas with you at your family villa, only to find that it didn't belong to you.'

'Now, not only have I got to pay for my own accommodation, but you want me to pay your bills as well? You are begging me for money to stop you being thrown out!'

'I didn't exactly invite you. I said you would be welcome if you did come. And you were!' Cara said hotly. 'I didn't know my father was having another crisis. And I'm asking for a loan, that's all.' There were tears in her eyes. 'I thought you came here because you wanted to be with me. Now, it's obvious that you just wanted a cheap holiday!'

They glared at each other, and then Geoff stood up abruptly, knocking his chair over. He made no attempt to pick it up. but stalked out of the room.

Cara put her elbows on the table and rested her head on her hands. Tears ran down her face. She did not know if she was crying because her dream of a life with Geoff was clearly finished, or whether they were tears of anger at the way he had reacted to his discoveries.

She wiped the tears away. Life had to go on. What could she do now?

At that moment the door opened and Margaret the travel rep came in, her normally good-humoured expression replaced by a frown.

'Your friend Geoff came marching out and nearly knocked me over,' she complained. 'He didn't even stop to apologise.' She looked at Cara. 'Oh, dear. A lovers' quarrel?'

'Not lovers, not any more,' Cara told her flatly. 'I'm sorry for his bad behaviour, though.'

'I've had worse,' Margaret said philosophically. She spotted the fallen chair and went to pick it up. 'It looks as if you've had a really nasty scene. Is there anything I can do?'

Cara suppressed the urge to tell the motherly woman everything. After all, she did work for a travel company, and couldn't be expected to sympathise with guests who came to the hotel knowing very well that they might not be able to pay their bill. If only her mother had been completely honest with her they would have been back in England in her house now, probably arguing, but not in debt, and she wouldn't have lost Geoff.

'I'm afraid not,' she said instead, unwilling to see the kindly expression of concern be replaced by disgust. 'It was just one of those things. I'll be fine, don't worry.'

'Well, if you do need help or someone to listen, come to me. I know you aren't here with my company, but I like you and your mother, so you can regard me as a friend.'

'I'll remember that,' Cara said with a grateful smile, and left the room to find her mother.

7

As Mrs Dale chatted to other guests, Cara sat by the pool. There was a book open on her lap, but she read very little of it. It seemed to her that life couldn't get any worse. She'd lost Geoff, that was clear, and tomorrow the hotel would present a bill that neither she nor her mother would be able to settle.

She was angry with herself — for agreeing to come with her mother in the first place, for not going home as soon as they'd learned the house was not theirs, and for misleading Geoff.

If only she had insisted on sticking with her original plan, she would have been spending a quiet, pleasant holiday with Geoff in London.

Then she remembered that, if she had refused to come to Spain, her mother might have ended up having to cope with all the problems in Spain by herself. Her anger turned towards her parents. They had been happy with their way of life, but they did not seem to realise the traumas she had had to endure as a result, and now they seemed to be in a financial mess from which there was no way out and which was entangling her.

And as for that silly scene with Nick and Lily!

The day dragged slowly to an end. Neither Lily nor Geoff were to be seen and Nick hardly spoke a word when he appeared with his mother, so their table at dinner was almost silent.

Cara went up to their room early, claiming she had a headache, which was true. When her mother came up she was in bed but lay with her eyes closed, pretending to be asleep. She heard her mother in the bathroom, but then she felt her mother's weight on her own bed.

'Open your eyes, Cara. We need to talk.'

Reluctantly Cara struggled up to a sitting position, propped against her pillow. She feigned surprise.

'Tell me what's the matter.' Her mother's voice was coolly determined.

'Nothing. I just have a headache.'

'For heaven's sake, Cara, I'm not stupid! Yesterday you were as happy as anything, and today you are sullen and miserable. I get the feeling that you are blaming me for whatever it is that's changed your mood.'

Cara gazed ahead, refusing to meet her mother's eyes.

'Geoff has found out about the house. He went there and talked to the people who are staying there, and knew something was wrong. So I had to tell him what had really happened.'

Her mother gave an impatient exclamation.

'Silly man! Why did he have to pry? He was being given a free holiday in a comfortable hotel — why couldn't he just have been grateful?'

'You don't understand. I told him everything. I told him that we might not be able to pay the hotel bill.'

Her mother was silent for a while.

'I can see how that would upset him. Your Geoff cares a lot about money, and he must have been horrified to hear he might have to pay for his own stay.'

Cara fidgeted.

'Well?' her mother demanded.

'I did think he might help. I suggested he might lend us some money . . . '

'And?' she urged.

'He just walked out,' she confessed miserably.

'I'm not surprised!'

She looked at Cara sideways.

'I don't suppose he'll reconsider, will he?'

'No.' There was no way.

'Oh. Well, we'll just have to see what happens.'

Cara could restrain herself no longer.

'But it's all your fault — yours and Father's! If you hadn't dragged me out here Geoff and I would have been perfectly happy together in England. It's always been the same. You and

Father have disrupted my life a dozen times, and you just don't seem to realise the harm you're doing!'

Mrs Dale's eyes opened in shock.

'Harm? We've always tried to do our best for you! If we had bad luck sometimes, that wasn't our fault. We didn't do such a bad job as parents. After all, look at you now. You have a good job and a house of your own. You wouldn't have those if you had been used to getting everything you wanted easily, if you hadn't fought for them. And now you're sorry for yourself because you've lost Geoff, who seems to care for money more than he cares for you.'

'He was everything I've always wanted! Steady, dependable, financially secure, good-looking!'

'He was dull, dull, dull, Cara! And smug and self-satisfied. I didn't criticise him much, because I thought you were really fond of him, but now he's gone I have to say I'm glad!'

Too furious to reply, Cara thumped

her pillow into place and lay down. She turned away from her mother and closed her eyes, feigning sleep.

After a minute she heard her mother get into bed and then the light clicked off. It was a long time before Cara could really sleep.

★ ★ ★

The next morning, the two women, both pale and heavy-eyed, avoided looking at each other as they got washed and dressed.

Mrs Dale broke the silence.

'Well, today's the big day. I wonder where we will be sleeping tonight.'

Cara swung round, almost in tears, her fists clenched.

'Aren't you worried at all?'

Her mother sank down on her bed.

'Of course I'm worried! I'm scared! I don't know what to do and I wish your father was here.'

'Because you think he will miraculously solve our problems?'

'Because he'd try — and because I love him and miss him!'

Now she was crying, big tears rolling down her cheeks. Cara was instantly across the room and comforting her mother in her arms.

'Don't! I'm sorry! It's just that you always seem to hope for the best while I fear the worst.'

Mrs Dale sniffed, fumbling for a tissue.

'I may seem like that, but I assure you that quite often in the past I've been scared stiff, but I didn't want to frighten you, and I didn't want your father to think that I didn't have complete faith in him. I know he's got us into some awkward situations in the past, but when he took risks it was always because he wanted to be able to give us more. It's just that, sometimes, he got a little over-ambitious.'

She sniffed again.

'Come on, let's tidy ourselves up and go down to breakfast. Crying makes me hungry.'

'We'll go and see the manager together this afternoon and explain everything to him. I'm sure he will be sympathetic,' Cara announced.

'If you say so, dear.'

There were signs at the table that two people had breakfasted early, and when Nick and his mother appeared it became clear that Geoff and Lily must have been avoiding the other members of the party. Nick caught Cara's eye and gave her a rueful smile. Cara found herself smiling back.

With possibly only a few hours left to enjoy the hotel's facilities, Cara decided on soothing exercise in the indoor pool, while her mother told her that she was going to see if the hairdresser had time free to attend to her. Gliding through the clear water of the pool demanded enough effort to stop Cara thinking of the awkward interview that afternoon with the hotel manager, and she stayed immersed in the water longer than she usually did.

Then she showered and went to the

lounge, where she found Mrs Clarke having coffee on her own and not in a good mood.

'Nick has gone off by himself,' she informed Cara. 'I needn't tell you who he's going to see. And Lily hasn't been to see me for ages!'

Cara made suitably sympathetic noises while looking round for her own mother, who was nowhere in sight.

'I don't know whether to order coffee now or wait,' she said. 'Perhaps Mother had to wait for the hairdresser.'

'No, she wasn't there,' Mrs Clarke said positively. 'I've been having my hair done. Can't you tell?'

'I'll just go and look for her,' and Cara hurried away, leaving Mrs Clarke to wonder why everybody seemed to be avoiding her.

Cara finally found her mother sitting on one of the sun beds by the pool. She looked very small, huddled on the seat.

'Mother! What are you doing out here? There's a nasty wind and it's obviously going to rain again.'

Her mother looked up, and managed a travesty of a smile to welcome her worried daughter.

'I was going into the lounge, but then I decided I just wanted some time by myself.'

Cara sat down beside her.

'What's happened?' she said apprehensively.

'I went to see the manager. I know you said we would go together this afternoon, but I got you into this mess, after all, so I thought I should be the one to face him.'

'What happened?' Cara asked flatly.

'Well, there were difficulties. First we tried my credit card, but that was rejected. Insufficient funds again. So then we talked — or I talked and he listened for most of the time.'

She looked up at Cara.

'I pointed out that the Christmas holidays meant that transactions might not have been processed by the banks as quickly as usual. I told him that he would get his money eventually, even if it took some time and we had to pay it in instalments. I tried a little gentle blackmail by pointing out that of course we would tell all the friends we had made here that we were being thrown out with nowhere to go.

'It took some time, but it's all right. We can stay at the hotel till the day after New Year's Day.'

Cara realised she had been holding her breath and let it out with a whoosh of relief. They wouldn't have the humiliation of being made to leave.

'Thank heavens for that! By then my salary will be in the bank and we'll be able to afford flights home, though I'm not sure I'll be able to pay all the hotel bill.'

'I told you everything would be all right,' her mother said, but there was something about her tone that made Cara look at her sharply.

'What's the matter?' She was suddenly alert to her mother's lost look.

'I want to know where your father is. What is he doing? Is he all right?'

'Don't worry. We'll hear from him soon.'

'But I can't help worrying. He's never lost contact with me for so long before, ever!'

Her hand went up to her neck in a familiar gesture, but for the first time Cara realised that there was nothing for her to grasp. Her mother's gold chain was gone.

'Where's your necklace?'

Her mother shrugged.

'The manager wanted some security, and that was all that I could offer.'

'But you've always had that chain! Whatever else changed, you always had that.'

'Yes. Your father gave it to me when you were born. It's the one thing I've never parted with — until now. But it's only a necklace, after all.' She sprang up, fists clenched. 'When your father does appear I'll make him suffer for what he's putting us through!'

'I'll help you,' Cara said grimly. 'Meanwhile, it's lunch time.' She bit her lip. 'I wonder if Geoff or Lily will appear this time.'

In fact, neither appeared, but Nick was there with his mother. His visit to his father must have been a brief one, and from his expression she could guess that it had not been particularly enjoyable.

At the end of the meal the two older women moved into the lounge for coffee. Cara was about to follow them when she felt Nick's hand on her arm, bringing her to a halt.

'Are you willing to skip coffee and come for a walk?' he asked. 'I think we could both do with a sympathetic listener this time.'

Cara was glad to be able to slip away and leave the two mothers to discuss the coming New Year celebrations. She and Nick made for the coast road which climbed gently to a headland with impressive views.

Nick walked along moodily, his hands thrust in his pockets. When he kicked a stone irritably out of his way he momentarily looked like a bad-tempered teenager, and Cara was reminded yet again of the difference in their ages.

At the top of the rise they sat on the low sea wall, staring at the ocean.

'You first,' Nick directed her. 'What has happened to the gorgeous Geoff?' He looked quizzical, and she realised he had seen through Geoff.

'We quarrelled,' she said curtly, and Nick raised an eyebrow.

'Is that all? You don't have to tell me the reason, but you could give a bit more information. It must have been a big quarrel if he is still sulking. Do you think there is any chance that you'll make it up and get together again?'

Cara shook her head vehemently.

'No chance. It's over.'

'Are you sorry?' His eyes bored into hers, as if trying to read her face.

'Of course I am!'

Then she stopped. Was she sorry? Wasn't there the tiniest sense of relief in the thought that she would no longer have to take care not to offend Geoff's sense of his own importance, would no longer have to listen to his word-by-word accounts of his successful dealings?

'I think I am,' she amended.

Nick was looking smug.

'That's more like it. I know he was good-looking and apparently successful, but he would have bored you silly.'

This echoed her mother's opinion too closely.

'He would have made a good husband,' she said stubbornly and Nick groaned aloud.

'I'm sure he would have looked after you and remembered your birthday and things like that, but can you imagine laughing at things with him, or making fools of yourself together and not caring? You're too eager to avoid risks, Cara. You're building a prison for yourself, missing out on the excitement and fun of life.'

'Maybe I had enough of that as a child . . . '

'Ah, yes. I've had the impression from your mother it's been an eventful life, so to speak.'

'I don't want a life like hers,' she admitted.

'Why not? She is happy. Isn't that what matters?'

Cara's shoulders slumped.

'I don't know. Anyway, forget about me, it's your turn now. Lily seems to have realised that you don't want her permanently. What's the situation with your father?'

Nick produced a sound between a sigh and a groan.

'I feel like a ball, being hit backwards and forwards between the two of them. Mother still refuses to speak to him, let alone consider a reunion, but now she wants to know everything he says and does. Dad is very hurt that his attempt at a dramatic reconciliation failed. He says she used to complain that he was too predictable, and then, when he tried to do something to surprise her, she just got upset!

'He's still in Nerja, and says he's going to stay there for a few days longer. I think he's hoping that she'll hear 'Auld Lang Syne' on New Year's Eve, remember all their years together, dissolve into tears and rush into his arms, happy ever after.'

'What do you think?'

'Not a chance! He left her, and he'll have to crawl if he wants to be taken back.' He shook his head.

'Do you want them back together again?'

'Yes. They had nearly thirty years together, and they were contented most of that time. They were good companions who could rely on each other. I know they both miss that, and the little things that went with it, the daily rituals that they both enjoyed. Mum doesn't like being on her own, and it may sound selfish but I'm not willing to move back in with her. I'm twenty-five, you know!'

'So, what are you going to do?'

'Keep going between them until

Mum decides he's suffered enough and it's time to forgive him.'

'You think that's likely?'

'It's possible.'

'Which is more than you can say about Geoff getting back with me.' She stood up. 'Come on. Let's get back to the hotel and be good children.'

As they went in the hotel, Margaret and Eileen, the two travel reps for the Clarke's holiday firm, were bent over their desk, conferring, and when they looked up and saw Cara and Nick they beckoned them over. Their smiles of greeting were a little strained.

'We've been given a letter for each of you,' Margaret told them, and Pat solemnly held an envelope out to Nick while Margaret gave another to Cara, who opened it and read it rapidly.

Eyes widening, she turned to Nick.

'It's from Geoff! He says he's leaving and going back to England. He says a lot of other things as well. I definitely won't be seeing him when I get back to England.'

'Mine's from Lily. She's going as well.'

'They both left about an hour ago. They went together, in a taxi to Malaga.' Margaret coughed significantly. 'In fact, though they may have been avoiding you two, they have been together most of the time for the past two days.

'Nearly all the time,' she added in a voice heavy with implication and hidden suggestion.

Cara broke in on these revelations as something occurred to her.

'Margaret, do you know what happened with Mr Ransom's bill? After all, my mother and I had invited him to stay here as our guest.'

Margaret's mouth curled upwards.

'Mr Ransom paid his bill. In addition, he also paid Miss Heyes's bill.'

Cara shut her eyes as a great wave of relief passed through her. Nick's frown began to turn into a smile, then into a laugh. He looked very relieved.

'Poor Geoff, charmed, caught and charged in a couple of days!'

'We've both been dumped,' Cara pointed out.

'Well, we're well rid of both of them and I wish them joy of each other! Cara, let's celebrate. Come into the bar and I'll buy you a drink.'

8

'To Geoff and Lily! May they be happy together and never trouble us again!' Nick raised his glass in the air.

Cara started to raise her own glass and then stopped.

'Hold on! A couple of days ago this was the man I was going to spend the rest of my life with!'

'And aren't you glad you're not?'

She thought for a while, and then raised her glass decisively.

'To Geoff and Lily!'

She handed him Geoff's letter.

'Read this.'

Cara, the letter began, *It has become clear to me that you have deceived me, and not only about your father. I thought you cared for me, but from what I have seen and from what Lily has told me, you and Nick Clarke have been concealing your true relationship.*

Lily and I both feel betrayed and have decided to leave so as to avoid any more embarrassing encounters.

It had been signed simply with his name, without any farewell salutation.

'What a pompous load of nonsense! Lily says almost the same, word for word, so they must have written the letters together,' Nick commented. 'Do you want it back?'

'No. Tear it up.'

Grinning, Nick tore the letter into pieces which he stuffed in his pocket.

She picked up her glass but then sat silent, frowning.

'What's the matter?'

'Well, maybe Geoff wasn't the ideal man for me. But time is passing. Where is my Mr Right? Where do I look next?' She laughed uneasily. 'You won't understand — you're young. You have plenty of time for girlfriends before you need to start worrying about settling down.'

'You're starting to treat me like a teenager again. I think that most people are looking for the man or woman who will make them happy for the rest of their life.'

'Perhaps.' She looked up at him. 'Are you sure you won't miss Lily?'

'My mother will. I won't.'

His voice was decisive, Cara thought. She grew pensive for a moment.

'I suppose it was wounded pride that made Lily get together with Geoff. She thought there was something between you and me, so she went after Geoff in revenge. After all, the two of you haven't much in common.'

'From what you've said, Geoff and I have one thing in common which is extremely important to Lily, which is, in fact, the reason she was pursuing me so hard. We are both financially well-off.'

Cara nearly dropped her glass.

'You? But you are just starting your career. You can't have saved much yet! Aren't you still paying off your student loan?'

Nick put down his glass and looked

at her with mock severity.

'You're doing it again — judging me purely by my age. For your information I didn't go to university, so I never had a student loan. I started at the tool-making firm, where I still work, when I was sixteen years old, and it was the right choice. The firm makes a lot of custom-built machinery, and it turned out that I have a gift for designing tools and adaptations! In fact, the firm has let me take out several patents on things I have designed, and some of them have been very profitable. I shall probably buy into the firm eventually and become a junior partner.'

He smiled happily.

'I've been very lucky. I've found a job which I enjoy and do well, and I'm being rewarded for it, which is even better!'

Cara gave him a long look and then pushed her glass towards him.

'In that case, you can buy me another drink!' She laughed.

'At least the barman thinks I'm old

enough to do that.'

'You are going to make some girl extremely happy.'

'Or some woman.' He looked at her in a strange way.

After they had finished their drinks they went to join their mothers. They told them about Geoff and Lily leaving, without going into details. The two older women were surprised, and Mrs Clarke was offended that Lily had gone without saying goodbye to her.

But both were more interested in discussing whether they wanted to join an excursion to Marbella or not.

'We could look at all the big yachts,' Cara's mother said, 'and we can look in the shop windows, even if we can't afford to buy anything there!'

Eventually it was agreed that it would be a pleasant way to pass a few hours, but as they prepared to find the reps and inform them of their decision, Nick's mobile phone rang.

He fished it out of his pocket and his lips tightened as he listened.

'I'll come at once.' He snapped the phone shut before turning to his curious mother.

'That was the manager of the hotel at Nerja. My father has been taken ill and they've sent for an ambulance. I'll get a taxi and go direct to the hospital. I'll let you know what's happening.'

Mrs Clarke gasped and clutched her son's arm.

'Andrew's ill? I'm coming with you.' She looked round wildly. 'Where's my handbag?'

Mrs Dale reached along the couch and handed it to her.

'Here. Do you want me to come with you as well?'

'No, but thank you. I'll be all right with Nick.' She turned to her son. 'Nick, don't just stand there. Please. Go and get us a taxi!'

As Nick hurried off his mother stood clutching her bag till he returned, which he did very quickly.

'There's a taxi at the door.'

He took his mother by the arm.

'Let us know what happens,' Cara told him and he nodded, too concerned with his mother to reply.

The Dales followed them to the door and saw them into the taxi.

'I'm sure everything will be all right,' was Mrs Dale's soothing goodbye.

She and Cara went back to the lounge and sank down.

'I thought this was supposed to be a quiet, restful Christmas,' Cara remarked gloomily.

'So far the worst hasn't happened. We found somewhere to stay when we lost the house, we have a roof over our heads for another couple of days, and Mr Clarke could just have a bad attack of indigestion. And you've got rid of Geoff.' Mrs Dale looked sideways at Cara. 'It's a pity this crisis has come up. Now Geoff and Lily have gone, you could have got to know Nick better. He likes you.'

'Glad to hear it.'

'No, Cara, I mean he *really* likes you.' Her tone made her meaning clear, but

Cara shook her head scornfully.

'He feels at ease with me because I'm older. I could be his aunt, or a friend of his mother. I'm too old for him to have any romantic ideas.'

'I think you're wrong.'

Just as they were finishing dinner that evening, Nick slid into his seat and gave them a tired grin.

'Nick! How is your father? Has your mother come back with you?' Mrs Dale enquired eagerly.

'Give me a second and I'll tell you everything, but I really need a drink first. It's been a tiring afternoon.' He looked at the wine menu and beckoned a waiter, then made what was clearly an admirable selection from the list.

They waited while the wine was brought and approved. Then Nick insisted on filling their glasses before he filled his own and drank gratefully.

'My father has food poisoning, and the hospital is keeping him in overnight. My mother is staying with him. I've to pack a bag for her, and I'll be grateful if you will help me. I don't want to leave out anything essential.'

'Of course,' Cara said warmly. 'Now, give us more details.'

'Let the poor lad have something to eat first,' her mother reproved her. 'Drink your wine.'

In order to keep down their hotel bill they had stopped ordering wine with their dinner, and both women appreciated being able to enjoy a glass as Nick ate hungrily. Finally he laid his knife and fork down on his empty plate and sat back. He paused for a moment, as if to get his thoughts in order.

'My father was staying at his hotel on a bed and breakfast basis. Yesterday evening he had a meal at a rather dodgy restaurant, ate some seafood, woke up this morning feeling very unwell indeed and collapsed in his bathroom. Fortunately, the maid found him and sent for help.'

He grimaced.

'He had an unpleasant time when he got to the hospital, but he seems to be recovering now, though he's feeling very weak.'

'And your mother?'

'By the time we got to the hospital he was tucked up in bed. The first thing Mother did was give him a good telling off for being so stupid when he knows he's got a sensitive stomach!' He grew serious. 'Then she burst into tears. Anyway, she decided it was her duty to stay with him.'

'What do you think will happen next?'

'I'm hoping that a few nasty germs will do what his romantic reappearance couldn't, and bring them together again. Now, let's finish up this wine and wish them well.'

Afterwards, they packed a small suitcase with toiletries and a change of clothes for Mrs Clarke. Nick thanked them before he went off.

'I wouldn't have had a clue about face creams and things like that.' He smiled. 'I'll keep you informed about how things are.'

★ ★ ★

The following day he'd apparently breakfasted early and then presumably gone to the hospital. The next time they saw him he was escorting his mother into the hotel. Mrs Clarke looked surprisingly bright and cheerful for someone who had been nursing a sick husband overnight. Mrs Dale and Cara hurried over.

'How is your husband?'

'Much better, thank you. In fact, he's back at his hotel.' She was unbuttoning her coat hurriedly. 'Are you going to lunch? I'll come with you.'

They hurried into the dining room, eager to hear her news.

'Well, as Nick probably told you, the silly man ate some prawns that had gone off. It was stupid of him, really, because he's always had a sensitive stomach and seafood has upset him before. The hospital looked after him very well. He's now back in his hotel room, but that's not really satisfactory as they don't serve lunch or dinner.'

She paused, beaming.

'So, as my room here is large, I asked this hotel to put another bed in it. Nick and I are going to collect Andrew and bring him back here with us this very afternoon.'

'And afterwards? When he's better?'

Mrs Clarke hesitated and blushed.

'Well, we have been talking a lot. He's admitted that he was stupid, that he needs me, and I've come to see that possibly I didn't pay enough attention to his problems. In short, we're back together again.'

She looked at her son.

'Of course, Nick's very happy about it. It cheered him up after losing Lily.' Her brow wrinkled and the petulant tone returned briefly. 'I still don't understand why she vanished.'

'Well, you don't need her any longer, and Nick will find someone else,' Mrs Dale said warmly. 'Now, is there anything I can do to help you?'

From then on, for the first time since she came to Spain, Cara was able to enjoy a period of restful self-indulgence. For the rest of that day and the next she swam, read, walked on the beach, and even enjoyed siestas in the afternoon. Quite often the swims and walks, though not the siestas, were shared by Nick.

Mrs Clarke, assisted occasionally by Mrs Dale, nursed and cosseted the convalescent Mr Clarke. Nick told Cara that his father was thoroughly enjoying himself.

'After six months of looking after himself, I think he feels his present situation was worth an upset stomach!'

Cara privately thought that Nick himself was very happy now. His parents' reconciliation meant that he was freed from the responsibility of looking after his mother. There was a new, light-hearted gaiety about him, and he made an agreeable companion who made her forget about Geoff and even the looming hotel bill.

For New Year's Eve the weather reverted to its former bad habits. Steady rain fell all day, but there was still an atmosphere of festivity and anticipation in the hotel. Cara and her mother recklessly treated themselves to a session at the hairdresser's salon and, like every other female guest, spent a long time choosing and readying what they would wear for the evening party.

Both had chosen long silk dresses, Cara's a brilliant blue and her mother's a glowing violet. They added accessories — shoes, belts and jewellery. Mrs Dale had rarely worn any other necklace than her gold chain, so borrowed a silver and amethyst necklace from Cara.

She fingered it a little wistfully.

'We'll get your chain back, Mother. Don't worry about it.'

'But I miss it. Whenever your father was away I used to feel that my chain was a link between us.' Mrs Dale thumped down a shoebox with unnecessary force. 'Why doesn't the stupid man get in touch? Even if it's to tell me that we've lost every penny as well as having nowhere to live, I want to know!'

Cara couldn't resist a giggle and her mother glared at her.

'I'm sorry,' her daughter said, 'and it isn't really funny, but I keep imagining the three of us living in my tiny little house.' She giggled again. 'As you said, you could do the cooking and housework while I go to work.'

'Forget that!' her mother replied, and then shrugged. 'Oh, well, I'll hear from him eventually, I suppose.'

As before, they were ready to enjoy life's little luxuries while they could and therefore went down for afternoon tea. It was quieter than usual, many guests deciding they needed a good afternoon's rest before the evening celebrations commenced.

The hotel manager was standing by the Reception Desk. He gave a polite bow and a small smile. Cara and Mrs

Dale smiled back rather nervously as they passed.

'Do you think he'll be as polite when he asks us to leave?' Cara murmured as they sat down.

They were joined by Mrs Clarke, then Nick, and drifted into idle small talk about the past few days.

'I never expected to be celebrating New Year's Eve with Andrew!' Mrs Clarke marvelled.

'Where is he?'

'I insisted that he had a good rest this afternoon. I think he'll be able to come down for the meal, but of course he won't be able to stay up and see the New Year in.'

They were distracted by sounds coming from the Reception area.

'I've been told that my wife and daughter are staying here.' A man's voice came loudly. 'Please call their room again and tell them I'm here.'

'I am afraid they're not answering. They must be somewhere else in the hotel,' was the reply.

'Then send someone to find them.'

Cara and Mrs Dale stared at each other, wide-eyed. They craned round to see who was speaking. Mrs Dale gave a little squeak, leaped to her feet and ran towards Reception.

'Bob!' she almost screamed.

The short, stocky little man in the black overcoat spun round as he heard her, and held out his arms just in time to catch her as she hurled herself at him. For a few seconds they held each other, and then Mrs Dale struggled free and faced the newcomer with her hands on her hips.

'Where have you been? Why didn't you let us know what was happening? Cara and I have had an awful time. First we had to get out of the house and we had to move in here, then we discovered that you hadn't paid my credit card bill, and we haven't even got enough to pay the hotel!' She waved a hand at the hotel manager, who had reappeared at the sound of raised voices.

The new arrival lifted his hands in mock surrender.

'I know, but things have been difficult for me, too. I'll explain everything later, but what's this nonsense about the hotel bill? And why aren't you staying at our house? I went there and was redirected here.'

'There is an outstanding bill,' the manager interrupted smoothly before Mrs Dale could embark on an explanation. He pressed a computer key and a print-out appeared as if by magic. 'Would you like to inspect it?'

Mr Dale gave the bill a brief second's glance, then turned to the manager.

'I assume you've got it right.'

He plunged a hand inside his overcoat, felt for something, and then pulled out a big wad of notes and began to peel off several hundred euro banknotes nonchalantly.

'How much do you want?'

The manager picked up the notes and counted them as they rained down on the counter.

'This is enough,' he said finally, his voice definitely warming.

'Good.' Mr Dale stuffed the remaining money back inside his overcoat and turned to hug Cara. 'Hallo, my darling.'

Then it was back to the manager.

'I want to stay here for a few days. What rooms have you got?'

'You're sharing mine, you idiot!' his wife interrupted. 'Cara, you're the one who needs a room.'

Ten minutes later everything had been sorted out. Mr Dale was to move in with his wife, and Cara would take the room which had been vacated by Lily and which was still empty.

'Well, now that's settled, I need a drink.'

'We were having tea, Father.'

He looked at his daughter with pity.

'Cara, I have finally been reunited with my wife and my only child after a long, lonely separation. And this is New Year's Eve. Order champagne, while I go up to our room and get rid of my coat and briefcase.'

He strode towards the lifts. Mrs Dale lingered by the desk for a few seconds more and held out a hand imperatively towards the manager, who nodded and went into his office. He returned with a small package which he handed to Mrs Dale, who snatched it and then hurried after her husband.

Cara went to the bar and ordered the champagne before returning to the lounge, where Mrs Clarke and Nick had witnessed everything, together with half the hotel.

'So that is the mysterious Mr Dale,' Nick commented. 'Is your father always like that?'

'Usually,' Cara admitted, sinking down into the cushions. Life was suddenly absolutely marvellous and she hadn't a care in the world.

The Dales returned just as the waiter brought the champagne in its ice bucket, and Cara saw that her mother's gold chain was once more round her neck.

Mr Dale was introduced to Nick and

Mrs Clarke. He shook their hands warmly, accepted them as if they were already old friends, and instructed the waiter to bring five glasses.

'Let's celebrate!'

9

Cara found herself carrying all her possessions between her old and new rooms instead of enjoying a leisurely bath before dressing. It took several trips in the lift, with a final dash to reclaim her toothbrush. However, a last look in the mirror before she went downstairs later with her parents showed that she was looking at her best. Her father's arrival and his thick wad of notes seemed to indicate that the financial crisis had passed, and she felt as if a physical weight had been lifted.

If Christmas Eve had been a big production by the hotel, New Year's Eve was completely over the top. Many local residents had come for the celebrations, some of the men in full evening-dress. Nick and Mr Dale wore formal suits with shirts and ties, though the ties soon disappeared as the temperature rose.

The meal was even longer and more elaborate than on Christmas Eve. There were party favours and jokes, and laughter and conversation almost drowned the sound of the trio of musicians patiently working through their thankfully updated repertoire.

Mrs Clarke had decided that her husband was well enough to be displayed to the other hotel guests, and he came to the dinner, his wife constantly fussing over him and telling him what he could and could not eat. He accepted her ministrations with apparent gratitude, though Cara wondered whether their reconciliation would be shaken by a few arguments once he had recovered his full strength.

Naturally, Mrs Clarke was extremely interested in Mr Dale's sudden appearance in Spain.

'And are you staying here with your family now?' was her first question. 'They missed you at Christmas. What a pity you couldn't be here then!'

'I missed them too,' was his brief reply.

After a few more attempts Mrs Clarke realised that her curiosity wasn't going to be satisfied and gave up her attempt to extract information.

After the meal came more music, and dancing. Cara's father insisted on dancing with his daughter.

'I hope you realise that I am as curious as Mrs Clarke,' she whispered as they circled the floor in a sedate waltz. 'I want to know what you have been doing, and precisely what the situation is now.'

'Don't worry. I've promised your mother that I'll tell you both everything tomorrow morning, but meanwhile I had to rush like mad to get here today and all I want to do this evening is enjoy myself. However, I will tell you that everything is going to be all right.'

So all of them settled down to enjoy the rest of the celebration. Nick and Cara, free of parental worries, spent a lot of the evening together, and just before midnight were out on a balcony enjoying a few quiet minutes in the fresh night air.

'Just look at them!' Nick said, pointing through the curtains to indicate his parents. 'I never dreamed this holiday would end so well.'

'Neither did I!' Cara said emphatically.

He looked at her questioningly.

'I sometimes got a hint that you were having difficulties,' he said, 'and not only with Gorgeous Geoff.'

'You were right. I'm not sure that I can tell you about them, but it seems the problems have been solved.'

'Good. So both of us can really make a fresh start with this New Year.'

Suddenly they were aware of a great roar from indoors.

'It's midnight! Happy New Year!' exclaimed Cara.

'And Happy New Year to you!' Nick said, and took her in his arms.

It started as a simple festive kiss, but

grew in passion and intensity. Cara felt as if the two of them were becoming one, her body aware of Nick's pressed close against her. She wanted the kiss to go on, to be able to just feel and not think.

She tried to tell herself that Nick was ten years younger than she was, so this should not be happening, and she started to struggle free. But, after all, she remembered that this was New Year's Eve, and everybody was free to kiss anybody they chose. She relaxed against him once more, but now it was Nick who drew away.

'Happy New Year,' he repeated flatly.

He bent forward to kiss her on the brow. Then, quickly, he took her hand and led her indoors, back to their parents who were still chattering nonstop.

It was the first night that Cara had had a bedroom to herself since her arrival at the hotel, and she did enjoy the privacy and freedom.

Perhaps there were compensations in

being single, she told herself, but when she fell asleep she dreamed of Nick's kiss.

★　★　★

As might be expected, both guests and staff at the hotel were tired and slow the next morning. Very few guests wanted to enjoy a full breakfast, and a skeleton staff yawned as they moved slowly through the restaurant. Cara ate alone, and then returned to her room until a telephone call summoned her to her parents' room, where both greeted her with a hug and more good wishes for the coming year.

'He's going to tell us everything now,' Mrs Dale announced.

Her husband held up a hand to his wife in mock supplication, laughing.

'I'm going to tell you the important bits. If I go into every detail we'll be here all day.'

'So what *are* the important bits?' Cara demanded. 'All we know is that, when we came out here to a house which you thought was yours and which turned out not to be, everything was going wrong. Now you've arrived with your pockets stuffed with cash, but is that all you've got? What happens next, Father?'

Her father sighed, held up his hands to silence their questions, and settled down into his chair.

'First of all, I'm very sorry about the villa. It seemed a reasonable transaction, and if I ever get my hands on the man who lied to me I will make him very sorry as well.

'However, you did the sensible thing. You came out here and waited to hear from me.'

'Except we didn't hear from you, so we just sat here and worried ourselves sick!' This was Mrs Dale.

'I'm sorry. I was very busy, and I didn't want to tell you one thing one day and then have to call you the next and say that circumstances had changed. I had to wait till I myself knew what was happening from day to day, don't you see?'

'Then tell us now!' Cara ordered.

Mr Dale put his fingertips together and stared at them, avoiding the eyes of his wife and daughter.

'I'm not proud of the situation I got into. Things started to go wrong, and I was losing money. As you know, this has happened to me before. But this time my judgement didn't seem to be working as well as usual, and I got scared and took unnecessary risks in the hope of a quick solution. Too many of them went bad, and in the end I had no resources to fall back on.

'So I went to an old friend. I've known him since we were young together and because I valued his friendship I always swore that I would never try to get him involved in any of my business dealings. However, I told him everything, and asked for help. I'm not sure what I expected — a cheque, some good advice, some tips about the market. But I got none of those.

Instead, he offered me a job!'

Mrs Dale gave a little scream and her husband looked at her with a wry grin, clearly enjoying the effect of his news.

'He said he knew that I had valuable skills, but he thought I needed other people to pull me back when I was going wrong. He said he could use my skills in some very tricky business dealings his firm was involved with. He would pay me a fee, and if things went well I would get a bonus.

'Well, to my surprise it worked out extremely well. Twice, other people tried to question what I was doing, so twice I nearly stormed out, but then I thought of the fee and stayed. Both times, it turned out that those people were right to be cautious. As a result, the deal went through beautifully. I got the fee, and a large bonus besides.'

'Is that the money you brought with you?' Cara asked.

'Yes. It's what was left after I'd paid off my debts.'

'And what happens when that money runs out?'

Now her father had a genuine smile.

'Cara, for the first time in my life I've got a job — a proper job. I even have a desk and an office!'

Mrs Dale was shaking her head.

'You with a job, working nine to five! I can't believe it!'

'It's not nine to five, my love. Sometimes it will be ten hours at a stretch, sometimes a couple of hours. Sometimes I'll be away for days. I'll be using the skills and knowledge I have gained over the years, but I'll be working with other people, so the responsibility will not be mine alone. There will be a system of checks and balances, and I'll get a regular salary and bonuses.'

'How do you feel about that, after all the years you've spent on your own, working for yourself?' Mrs Dale enquired anxiously.

He reached over and patted her hand.

'My dear, ten years ago I would have hated it. Now? I think I'm relieved. I suppose it's age finally creeping up on me, but I want us to have security. I don't want to reel from crisis to crisis any more.' His face lit up. 'And I've got a flat to take you home to! It belongs to the firm, and the rent's very reasonable, as well.'

'It sounds like a fairy-tale ending,' Cara said a little dubiously, and her father laughed.

'Oh, there will be difficulties! I'll chafe against the restrictions, and having to get my actions approved by others, and I'll be certain that I could make more money on my own. But then I'll think back to these past few weeks, and of my pay-cheque, and do as I'm told.'

There was no guarantee that that was what would happen, but it was enough for the moment. Mrs Dale announced that she was taking her husband to look round Nerja.

Cara decided instead that a long walk

by herself along the coast would give her a chance to think over the past two weeks, and possibly make some decisions about her own future.

The road led along the coast with the sea on one side and cliffs on the other. It had been closed to traffic since the recent heavy rains had brought some boulders tumbling down on the road surface, so on new Year's Day it was virtually deserted.

She walked briskly for some time, enjoying the physical activity and the peace, till she reached the headland where she stood for a while admiring the sea stirred by the breeze. This had been her first visit to Spain and she wondered whether she'd ever come again.

She hoped so. The scenery in the mountains had been magnificent and she knew that beyond them lay the historic cities of Granada and Seville which she'd love to explore.

Of course, it would be a great place for a honeymoon, but now Geoff had gone she wondered whether marriage was still a possibility for her. She was thirty-five, so perhaps a life on her own filled with friends and hobbies was what she had to look forward to. There were worse fates, after all.

★ ★ ★

She looked at her watch and was surprised to see how time had passed. If she hurried, she might get back in time to grab a little lunch before the restaurant closed. But she'd only gone a few yards when she heard her name being called and turned to see Nick waving at her. He had apparently just rounded the headland.

She waited while he ran to catch her up.

'Have you been getting away from parents as well?' was her greeting, and he nodded.

'They've started appealing to me whenever they have any differences of opinion,' he complained. 'They're only going to sort things out properly if the two of them discuss any problems by themselves, so I'm keeping out of the way as much as possible for the rest of the holiday, and then I can escape back to my flat.'

'Where is your flat?' Cara asked politely.

He told her and her eyebrows rose.

'But that's only five minutes walk from where I live!'

'Good. We'll be able to see each other whenever we like.'

Cara came to a halt. This hadn't been the response she had expected.

'Nick,' she said resolutely, 'I know we've enjoyed being here together, but a couple of kisses doesn't mean we should start seeing each other when we get back. I don't think there would be any point in that.'

'You mean, because I'm ten years younger than you.'

'Yes,' she said flatly.

He waved his hands as if trying to think of the right words.

'Cara, don't be so — silly, stupid, short sighted, old-fashioned . . . ' He hesitated, searching for more words while her cheeks flamed with anger.

'Why am I stupid?' she snapped. 'You are ten years younger than I am. That's a fact.'

'What difference does that make?'

'You haven't had much experience of the world, for a start.'

He looked at her levelly.

'I very much doubt that. My life has been lived to the full, while I get the impression you have been looking for safety, avoiding any experiences that might disturb your quiet life.'

'I am established in my career and financially secure!' she defended herself, uncomfortably aware he was right.

'Well, my career is also doing very well. In fact, one or two of my patents are already licensed world-wide.' He adopted a comical expression of pride.

'I don't want people to think I'm a cradle-snatcher!'

'Don't be daft! We're talking about

ten years, not thirty.' He took a deep breath. 'Cara, we're talking about all the reasons why we shouldn't get together, when we could be talking about why we should. From that first evening I found you very attractive, and as I saw more of you I found I liked you as well, and wanted to get to know you better.

'That was one of the reasons I was so furious when Lily turned up. I wanted to be with you, not her.'

'Haven't you ever heard of holiday romances? You'll soon forget me when we go back to England.'

'No, I won't. And, Cara, you need me. I can give you the financial security you wanted with Geoff, and I can also give you emotional security. You will be loved.'

His words stopped her momentarily. He seemed to be offering her everything she had ever wanted. But she tried to be realistic.

'For how long, Nick? Five, ten years? Then you'll look at me and regret that you're tied up to an older woman.' Her voice trembled in frustration.

'Why should I? Will your character change, or the way your eyes smile before your lips? The way you care about others?'

'When I'm fifty and you're forty . . . '

'Our children will be at school and I'll probably have taken up gardening, possibly even golf. I'll be settled and sedate, and you'll still be beautiful. Cara, you seem worried that I'll change my mind. But you haven't said anything about you getting tired of me. That gives me hope.'

This was going far too fast. She looked at him, part of her wanting to believe him.

'Children? You're already thinking of marriage? Nick, you seem to think I'm special. I'm not, and you'll realise that and be grateful when we get home and you don't see me every day.'

She turned away from him and began to trudge back towards the hotel, but suddenly there was a rumble and an agonised cry from Nick.

'Cara! Look out!'

She was seized bodily round the waist, lifted, and then hurled forward, landing spread-eagled on the ground as the rumble grew louder. Something heavy pinned her legs down. She struggled, dislodging the weight, and managed to look round. A section of the cliff had collapsed, sending a torrent of boulders and soil across the road. It had covered her legs, but if Nick had not rescued her she would have been completely buried under the main body of the landslide.

He sat up beside her and she turned towards him, badly shaken, and buried her head on his breast as he held her to him.

'You saved my life!'

'Of course I did. I love you.'

She lifted her head and his arms tightened round her and he bent to kiss her. The kiss seemed timeless, and all Cara wanted to do was stay there for ever, safe in his embrace.

'And, unlike last night, you didn't even remember that I'm ten years younger,' he murmured as he finally lifted his head.

She realised he had known very well what had been going through her head the last time they'd kissed.

'With my eyes shut, I couldn't tell,' she returned and he laughed, and then gazed into her eyes.

'Cara, you may be right. It may not work out with us. But you won't know unless you take a chance. You can play safe, but it could cost you a lifetime's happiness.'

She looked round and laughed helplessly.

'Nick, we're sitting in the middle of a road covered in earth and stones. Is this the time to decide what we are going to do with the rest of our lives?'

'Why not? Give me an answer. Will you take a chance?'

She lay in his arms and thought of her mother, who had spent her whole marriage taking risks, and who was definitely one of the happiest women she knew.

She thought of the Clarkes, whose marriage had broken down because it became too predictable. She thought of her relief when Geoff, her ideal match, had disappeared. Perhaps Nick had been right. She had spent so much of her life trying not to take any risks whatsoever, that she had missed out on all the excitement that involved.

Her decision was made without too much effort.

'All right, Nick, I'll take a chance. Now, will you let me go so we can get back to the hotel and clean up before lunch is over? I'm hungry and dirty!'

His grip grew tighter.

'Don't be so unromantic! Now, you said that when I was kissing you and your eyes were closed you forgot that I was ten years younger.'

She closed her eyes and lifted her face to his again . . .

We do hope that you have enjoyed reading this large print book.

Did you know that all of our titles are available for purchase?

We publish a wide range of high quality large print books including:
Romances, Mysteries, Classics
General Fiction
Non Fiction and Westerns

Special interest titles available in large print are:
The Little Oxford Dictionary
Music Book, Song Book
Hymn Book, Service Book

Also available from us courtesy of Oxford University Press:
Young Readers' Dictionary
(large print edition)
Young Readers' Thesaurus
(large print edition)

For further information or a free brochure, please contact us at:
Ulverscroft Large Print Books Ltd.,
The Green, Bradgate Road, Anstey,
Leicester, LE7 7FU, England.
Tel: (00 44) **0116 236 4325**
Fax: (00 44) **0116 234 0205**

Other titles in the
Linford Romance Library:

EARL GRESHAM'S BRIDE

Angela Drake

When heiress Kate Roscoe compromises herself through an innocent mistake, widower, Earl Gresham steps in with an offer of marriage to save her reputation. She is soon deeply in love with him, but is beset by the problems of overseeing his grand household. The housekeeper is dishonest and the nanny of the earl's two children is heartless and lazy. But a far greater threat comes from his former mistress who will go to any lengths to destroy Kate's marriage.

FINDING ANNABEL

Paula Williams

Annabel had disappeared after going to meet the woman who, she'd just discovered, was her natural mother . . . However, when her sister Jo travels to Somerset to try and find her, she must follow a trail of lies and deceit. The events of the past and the present have become dangerously entangled. And she discovers, to her cost, that for some people in the tiny village of Neston Parva, old loyalties remain fierce and strangers are not welcome . . .

IT WAS ALWAYS YOU

Miranda Barnes

Anna Fenwick is very fond of Matthew, a hard-working young man from her Northumberland village. She has known him all her life, although, sadly, it seems that he is not interested in her. Then Anna embarks on a whirlwind romance with Don, a visiting Canadian and goes to Calgary with him. Life is wonderful for a time. However, her heart is still in Northumberland — but when she returns to seek Matthew, will she eventually find him?

IN HER SHOES

Anne Holman

Inspector Mallison was reluctant to arrest the murdered man's son, although the incriminating evidence was overwhelming: he'd been alone with his father immediately prior to the murder and there'd been a bitter quarrel; Goldstein was killed trying to alter his will — unfavourably for his son; the weapon, a desk paperweight bore the son's fingerprints, and his father had withdrawn financial support for a new West End play in which his son was to star. Yet still Mallinson wasn't convinced . . .